The Two Ruths

Martha Emily Bellinger

Martha E Bellinger
7/15/21

ARCHWAY
PUBLISHING

Archway Publishing books may be ordered through booksellers or by contacting:

Archway Publishing
1663 Liberty Drive
Bloomington, IN 47403
www.archwaypublishing.com
1 (888) 242-5904

ISBN: 978-1-4808-5873-2 (sc)
ISBN: 978-1-4808-5871-8 (hc)
ISBN: 978-1-4808-5872-5 (e)

Library of Congress Control Number: 2018902252

Print information available on the last page.

Archway Publishing rev. date: 02/27/2018

To my "lesbian sisters" who lived in complete secrecy before the age of gay rights, but nevertheless served their communities and churches with distinction, while sharing the love and support of their equally remarkable partners at home.

Acknowledgments

I wish to thank my partner of thirty-four years, Pam, from whom I have learned that partnership will last even during the slings and arrows of life, if you keep on hugging. My "adopted" spiritual sister and former executive secretary, Esther, believed in this story and carefully proofread each page. My dear friend of fifty-three years, Marilyn, has always believed in my ability to write. At the innocent age of sixteen, I promised I would one day write a novel and send it to her. I hope it was worth the wait.

But Ruth replied, "Don't urge me to leave you or to turn back from you. Where you go I will go, and where you stay I will stay. Your people will be my people and your God my God. Where you die I will die, and there I will be buried. May the Lord deal with me, be it ever so severely, if anything, but death separates you and me."

—Ruth 1:16–17

Chapter 1

August 1950

Standing at her father's grave, Ruth's thoughts drifted back to 1926, when she was six. It was the first time she had left the family farm for a day to attend school. As tears streamed down her cheeks, she remembered how her father had walked her the two miles to the one-room schoolhouse that day. As he'd let go of her hand, he had said, "Now, I expect you home right after school, Ruthie, so you can help me get those cows milked. You know the way home, don't you, honey?"

Ruthie remembered trying to be brave and trying not to cry. "Yes, Father, you know I will be there. I love working in the barn with you. I don't know why I need to go to school," she had replied.

"Now, we have been all over that, Ruthie. It is a compulsory requirement of the state of New York that you go to school. Do you know what compulsory means?" her father had asked.

Ruthie had nodded her head in the affirmative and told her father that she thought it meant mandatory. She remembered her father beaming when she came back with that answer.

Her father had continued to explain, "Yes, compulsory and mandatory mean you are required to go to school. I also want you to remember that, even though you are a girl, you will not get anywhere in this world unless you know how to write decent and do some simple figuring. Even when you get married, something might happen to your husband, and you would be all on your own in the world, with maybe a whole raft of kids to look after. Being ignorant won't help you get them raised proper. You understand?"

"Yes, Father," Ruthie had replied sadly. "I will try to do a good job at school for you."

"I am sure you will, Ruthie. I told your mom when you were four that you caught onto things faster than any little child I'd ever seen. When you fixed a bicycle chain all by yourself last year with no help from me, I knew you were special. You have never given your mom or me anything but pride when you have sung songs with that sweet, pitch-perfect voice before the whole church without missing a word. So, you will catch onto the reading and writing real fast. I figure, after you graduate from high school, you can better decide what you want to do with your life."

"I should be real big by then, and I can help you a whole bunch more with those cows," Ruthie had stated with some confidence.

"I'm lookin' forward to that, Ruthie, if you don't find yourself some beau first and get all crazy in love." Her father had smiled broadly as he pinched Ruthie's cheek.

"I don't think that will happen, Father. All I want to ever do is farm!" Ruthie had exclaimed.

"Well, you have a special touch with those Holsteins, that's for sure. Never seen them take to anyone like they do to you. I guess they understand that, just like they have four stomachs, you have four hearts, all the time figuring out how to best make them happy," her father had replied with pride.

As the preacher proclaimed, "Dust to dust, ashes to ashes, we now commit the body of Walter Frank Stein to his eternal rest with our Lord, Jesus Christ, who has promised us that he was going before us to prepare a place for us when life was done," Ruth snapped back to reality.

Her beloved father was gone. She did not let out a sound, but tears poured down her face. She had to be strong for her mother. Who would have thought that her father would be gone before her mother? Alma Stein had endured a very bad heart condition for many years, and Ruthie had assumed her mother would be the first to go. God knew best, because Ruthie understood her father could not have survived her mother's death. She knew her father had adored her mother more than any other man who had ever loved his wife. He had never failed to kiss her when he came in from the barn after the nightly chores. He had always been careful to remove his coveralls in the garage and change out of his dirty shoes into his slippers before entering the house. It was the German way, she thought, to keep the house neat and clean. And Lord knew Mother would get upset over unnecessary dirt in the house.

It was curious to her that, while her father had always complimented her mother on her dress, her cooking, and her thriftiness, proclaiming he was "the luckiest guy in all upstate New York" to have made Alma his wife, her mother never seemed to return the compliment or even smile. She knew being a farmer's wife had been a difficult task for her mother, a young, small woman with a very fair complexion and the daughter of a dry goods merchant who had pampered his daughter most of her childhood.

It must have been her father's movie-star good looks that had turned her mother's head. Her aunt had once told her that her father was the most handsome man for miles around. There hadn't been a single woman within twenty miles who didn't dream of becoming his wife at the time he had chosen Mother. Farming had taken some toll on those looks, but despite the weather-beaten face, you could see the vestiges of a remarkably handsome gentleman. Yes, her father was always a gentleman and treated everyone with kindness. How could she ever go on without his endless stories and jokes, which seemed to lighten up any room he entered?

The burial rites having been completed, Ruthie took her mother by the arm and gently guided her out of the cemetery on what had turned out to be the perfect August day in 1950. The cemetery overlooked a large pond where ducks and geese frequently gathered. She looked out upon the pond today and saw a lone swan flapping its wings violently as it stood on the one small island in the pond. She remembered that her father had always told her swans were among the few animals that mated for life and that man should take notice of nature's intent that mates stay together. This swan was all alone and obviously gravely disturbed by the mate's absence. Suddenly, she got it: Father was sending a message that Mother was all alone now, and Ruthie had better take care of her.

"How are we ever going to survive now, Ruthie?" her mother sobbed.

"Well, Mother, we are going to do what we did the day Father died and every day since. I will get up as I always have and take care of the farm chores. When you feel up to it, you can make us some breakfast, just like you did for Father. And we will keep doing that every day, just as he would have wanted us to do. And as Father would have said, "The good Lord will watch over us because he is our shepherd, and we shall not want.""

"Now, Ruthie, I know you mean well," whined her mother, "but women were not meant to be farmers all by themselves. Even though your father said you were the strongest woman he had ever seen, it's just not right for you to be tied down like this, and it is well past the time you thought about dating or perhaps going to school to be a teacher or secretary. That is proper work for a woman, not farming. If only Walter Junior were here. Why did he have to land on Omaha Beach? I just about lost all my faith the day the man from the army pulled up to our front door and handed the telegram to your father. It's a wonder your father didn't have a stroke right then. At least if Walter Junior was here, he'd know what to do about this farm."

Ruthie was stunned by her mother's statement about Walter Junior. Yes, he was her older brother by two years, but their father had always had to urge Walter Junior to do his farm chores. Surely their mother knew this. Her brother had once said to Ruthie that he had no intention of staying around these parts and farming the rest of his life away. He knew that was what his father planned for him. But he was the first to grab *Look* magazine from the mail each month and read it cover to cover before sharing it with anyone else in the family. Having inherited his father's good looks, Walter Junior had dated about every single woman within twenty miles, but he kept them all on a string. He seemed to delight in the fact that so many of them wanted to marry him, but he was not ready to settle down in Four Corners.

At the dinner table, he would talk on and on about some new location in the world he wanted to see, to which her father had responded more than once, "Won't be much time for traveling once you soon take over this farm, son. Cows must be milked twice a day, and they just don't take to strangers milking them. Might be best you pick out one of those gals you've been dating, get married, and settle down on this farm."

They had been told by the army that Walter Junior had died most admirably on Omaha Beach. He had been part of the very first wave to hit the Normandy beach on June 6, 1944. It had been reported by a surviving member of his platoon that Walter Junior had been dragged under the water trying to save a fellow soldier who was floundering in deep water after being dispatched from the landing craft quite short of the actual sand. His Purple Heart and Bronze Star had been properly displayed on his mother's hutch for the past six years.

Ruthie remembered clearly the conversation Walter Junior had had with his parents when he'd signed up for the army. He was twenty-three years old at the time of Pearl Harbor, and like tens of thousands of other young men, Walter Junior had sought the nearest recruitment office and enlisted in mid-December 1941 before telling his folks. When he got home in time for dinner, he explained his absence from nightly chores by reporting that he was going to show the world that "patriotic German Americans were ready to save the world from crazy Japs and the relentless Fuhrer. After all, how would it look for a man named Stein to wait to be drafted?"

Ruthie never doubted her brother's patriotism. She also knew Walter Junior was happy to have an excuse to get away from the farm.

Nevertheless, she was truly proud of her brother, and since his death, she tried to keep her parents' minds off their loss by driving them to every church social and town meeting in the community. She would not let them stay home and mope around. As usual, it was easier to convince her father that life moved on and that, while Walter Junior's death was terrible, he had died a man caring for a fellow soldier, which was something she knew her father would have done under the same circumstances. Forevermore, the Stein family name would become even more honorable when people saw the military medals in their home and inquired about how they had come to be there.

Ruthie thought about the last three months before her father died. The very day he had his stroke she had gone out into the barn and done all the milking and feeding of the cows. She was amazed how quickly she could get the work done by herself. No doubt her father had slowed her down as they had done chores together those last few months. She would be milking one of the cows, and her father would yell for her. "Ruthie, can you empty this milking machine for me? My back's acting up again."

Ruthie would put down her own milking machine and race to her father's side to help him empty the heavy container. As quick as she was in responding to his call, in recent months, his hands would shake uncontrollably and sweat would pour down his face. She would also carry all his milk to the milk house, in addition to milking her half of the herd and emptying her own machines of milk into buckets, which were then carried to the large cans in the milk house. She had known it would be quicker to just milk the whole herd herself, but she didn't want to hurt her father's pride. It meant so much to him to do this work and talk about it at the dinner table while her disinterested mother pretended to listen. Ruthie had never reported her father's deteriorating health condition to her mother because she knew her mother would insist upon selling the farm immediately. The Stein land was some of the best in Jefferson County and would command a pretty penny.

"Now look, Mother, one day at a time; like Father always said, one day at a time. I love the farm chores; you know that. I always have, and I always will. You know I can do them pretty much all by myself. I have done that for three months since Father's stroke. Billy Packer comes over to help me with baling the hay and stacking it away in the haymow. Now he's promised to help me with the corn silage too, if I do the same for him. We got it all arranged."

"Well, maybe for now we can get by, Ruthie. But it does not seem right that a woman be running a farm mostly by herself, even if it is you," Mother responded glumly.

"Right—what is right, Mother? Working hard each day with God's creatures and providing milk and food for our neighbors, isn't that right, Mother? Doesn't everyone know I worked this farm side by side with Father for years after high school? They won't find it strange if I carry on in that matter. They know how Father always said he thought his daughter had a special way with the Holsteins and knew farming better than any ten boys you'd meet in this part of the county," Ruthie reassured her mother.

If ever God created a woman for dairy farming, it was Ruthie. She stood just two inches short of six feet, one inch taller than her father. She was a husky 185 but with muscles as hard as rocks. She easily handled 40-pound bales of hay and threw them about with little trouble. More than once she had put a newborn calf that had been born in the field on her shoulders, carrying the calf all the way back to the barn. Despite her tomboyish appearance, Ruthie had sparkling hazel eyes that flooded forth with kindness. She always managed a smile for everyone, while hiding a slight sadness of feeling alone in the world. She had never met anyone like herself, but she never questioned why God had put her on the earth. She needed no other purpose in life but this small farm of a hundred acres, which had provided a steady, if humble, existence for the Stein family for over a hundred years.

As Ruth guided her mother to their 1939 Ford, she was approached by Billy Packer. "Ruthie, John and I are going to do your milking for you tonight if you will let us. We'd like to give you a chance to be with your mother this evening without thinking about the farm for once," Billy pleaded.

Before Ruthie could open her mouth, her mother chimed in, "Well, that would be wonderful, Billy. Don't you think that is so nice of our neighbors, Ruthie?"

"Yes, Mother, that is very nice of them to offer to do the milking, but I am perfectly capable of doing it. It is what Father would have wanted me to do tonight," Ruthie replied.

"Your father would have wanted you to look after me, Ruthie, this one night of all nights. My heart doesn't feel very strong this evening. I think having you in the house would comfort me considerably," Mother insisted.

"Well, I guess that decides that, Billy, and I will try to find some way to return the favor soon," Ruthie replied.

"You've already done more things for me and my family than I could ever do for you were I to live to be a hundred, Ruthie. All the vegetables from your garden you gave us when my parents were so sick with influenza, the nights you sat by my mother's bed and saw her through the high temperatures and coughing spells. I haven't forgotten that, Ruthie."

"That's just what neighbors do for one another," Ruthie replied. "After all, if we don't look out for one another out here in the middle of nowhere, who's going to?" Ruthie responded.

"You know you were the only person for miles around who didn't fear catching influenza, Ruthie, while taking care of Mama."

Even though that was some time after the Spanish flu, which had taken her own grandparents in 1919, Ruthie clearly remembered how people were scared nearly to death about a new epidemic.

"You were downright heroic when it came to my mother, and I will never forget that." Billy spoke loudly so everyone around could hear.

It was difficult for Ruthie to take compliments. She didn't know why, but she hated to have attention drawn to her in any way. She preferred to be like the old draft horse they had kept on the farm when she was a little girl. Just keep the head down and move forward with whatever load had to be carried. She hurried her mother into the Ford and drove home to the farmhouse five miles away.

Chapter 2

They rode in silence back to the house. Ruthie's mother had never been one to initiate much conversation with anyone. She had left that up to her husband, who was always completely at ease with whomever happened to be around. Ruthie was surely a combination of her parents' dispositions. She always had a friendly smile for everyone but always hung back just a bit, not quite sure what to say or how to say it. Ruthie thought about how tough it would be now without her father. It wasn't the farm chores she dreaded or keeping stock of the accounts or even having farm equipment fixed when it was needed. She could do all those things. But she was not her father's equal in the conversation department and had always relied upon him to speak for her when they were in the presence of others, particularly in the presence of her mother.

Communicating with others had come so easily for her father. Ruthie often stood back in amazement as she watched her father tell some joke or story that had a whole room full of strangers laughing within minutes of meeting him. Even when she had heard the same story before, she never failed to laugh, just considering how positively her father affected others. When it came to her mother, she had always relied upon her father to speak up for her if need be or at least keep a conversation flowing. She was now faced with the reality that she would have to find some way to carry on a normal conversation with her mother without having it seem strained or forced. She had always felt very uncomfortable around her mother, always feeling that, somehow, she just hadn't become the type of daughter her mother wanted. When Walter Junior was killed on Omaha Beach, Ruthie always suspected her mother had wished Ruthie had been another son who had sacrificed his life for America. As they continued their silent ride back to the farm, Ruthie reflected to a time in her late teen years when she had come into the house from the barn wearing her usual coveralls and one of her father's flannel shirts. Her mother had looked her up and down and said, "It is just too bad, Ruthie, that God didn't make you into a boy. I swear you would have been happier." Her mother's scornful comment had stung Ruthie greatly, but she had said nothing back. She wished she felt comfortable all dressed up in pretty dresses and skirts, but the fact was she didn't, and such attire was not very practical around a farm anyway.

When they got back from the cemetery, they walked inside the farmhouse and were met by two members of the Methodist Women's Fellowship who had filled their whole dining room table with casseroles, as well as delicious-looking desserts and breads.

"Alma and Ruthie, we didn't want you to have to worry about cooking for a while. The two of you have been so faithful to our fellowship this was the least we could do," Mrs. Hodge said.

"You can decide what you want to eat tonight and put the rest in the icebox for tomorrow and the next day," added Mrs. Reynolds.

"Why, that is so wonderful, ladies. Truth is I don't feel much like cooking tonight, and cooking is not Ruthie's best suit as you know, though Lord only knows I've tried to turn her into a decent cook," Ruthie's mother commented.

Mrs. Hodge and Mrs. Reynolds looked at Ruthie with half smiles, both having overheard some hurtful comments by Mrs. Stein to her daughter, which they thought were totally unnecessary. They had talked before about how Mrs. Stein seemed unaware that Ruthie had needed her mother's approval and that Ruthie was owed that approval. They had always liked Mr. Stein better than his wife, and they knew that Ruthie was the apple of her father's eye. Thank God Mr. Stein had always bragged about his daughter's accomplishments to others. They often wondered if Mrs. Stein was just jealous of her own daughter, insofar as she seemed to make Mr. Stein happier than his own wife of forty years.

Mrs. Hodge and Mrs. Reynolds looked at one another and smiled, and then Mrs. Hodge spoke up again. "Well, even if Ruthie was the finest cook on earth, we don't think she should be cooking tonight. We know how much you loved your dad, Ruthie, and we are so sorry he died at fifty-eight. That is just too young, Ruthie. Thank goodness you still have your mother."

"Well, yes, that is quite right," Ruth politely responded. "I'll try to make sure I thank the good Lord every night for mother's presence in my life each day."

"Yes, well we're going to leave the two of you alone to eat and rest," added Mrs. Reynolds. The two elderly but spritely ladies gave both Alma and Ruthie a hug and departed quietly.

It was not quite dinnertime yet, but Ruthie knew her mother had eaten practically nothing for breakfast. And so, she inquired, "Mother, are you hungry? I think some of these casseroles are still hot, and if you want one that isn't, I can heat it up for you?"

"No, Ruthie, I have no appetite. I think I am just going to go upstairs and lie down for a bit. It has been a hard day for me, Ruthie. Your father and I were together for forty years as you know. Every night when we went to bed, he would always kiss me and thank me for what I had done that day. Then he would settle back on his pillow and invite me onto his shoulder. I would usually fall right asleep, and when I would wake up early in the morning before he got out of bed to do the morning chores, I would find his hand in mine. That is what I will miss the most, Ruthie, that strong hand holding mine." A tear rolled down her mother's cheek, and then her mother turned and struggled upstairs to what had been her parents' bedroom.

Ruthie felt her eyes well up with tears. Why wouldn't a wife be devastated to lose the best husband God had ever created? Although it was really the last thing she wanted to think about tonight, she knew that, if she married, she would try to show the same affection to her husband that her father had given unconditionally all those years to her mother. Even when her mother was complaining about some little thing of no consequence, Father just smiled and said, "Yes, Alma." Ruthie knew she needed to forgive her mother for the less-than-affectionate demeanor she had often displayed toward her father. Her father wanted so little for himself of a material nature. He just wanted love. Ruthie had observed the fading smile from her father's face each time he had given many compliments to her mother in the presence of others, which were never returned, not even with a slight smile.

Ruthie had instinctively given her father much praise. Even if she felt she needed to make up for her mother's sometimes very selfish behavior toward her father, her compliments were always sincere and based upon good deeds by her father. Ruthie picked up the social graces taught by her mother because her mother would complement and be thankful to others for what they had done for her—even if she couldn't find it within her heart to do the same toward her own family.

When she was a very little girl and her father had taken her to town on some farm errands, he'd always go into the five-and-dime and buy a little bag of penny candy for his daughter. Ruthie had little trouble expressing her gratitude by saying, "Thanks, Daddy." That always brought a smile to his face. Whenever she would come home with a report card full of A's with her father marveling at her intelligence, Ruthie would say, out of earshot of mother, "if I didn't have a smart father, I'd have never gotten these grades. I was just doing what you told me to do my first day of school—doing my best for you, Dad."

She thought, *Dear God, help me to let go of this anger I have in my heart for Mother. She is not perfect, but who am I to judge? Father loved her, so that is all that matters. He would want me to take care of her without complaint and that is what I will do.*

The next few months were very trying emotionally and physically for Ruthie. Her mother's health was failing. She could see that more and more as every day passed. Frequently, she would come into the farmhouse from the barn after the morning milking to find her mother still sleeping. This was so unlike the Alma Stein she had known for the past three decades.

Her mother had always been an early riser, often getting out of bed within a few minutes of her husband so she could prepare for the big breakfast she would make for him, as well as plan the rest of the day's meals. As a child, Ruthie had always awakened to the wonderful smells of percolating coffee; fresh baked bread; and, when in season, her favorite smell of all, those huckleberry muffins. When Ruthie got old enough to join her father and Walter Junior for morning farm chores, she would hear her mother dressing as Ruthie put on her overalls to go to the barn.

In the last few weeks, Ruthie would get all the morning barn chores completed and then clean up in the garage before entering the kitchen to make breakfast for herself and her mother. She had learned how to make good scrambled eggs, oatmeal, and a good pot of coffee. She had worked out an arrangement with Mrs. Packer to trade some eggs each week for some of her loaves of bread. She would get all the breakfast underway and then gently awaken her mother, helping her into a housecoat and to the breakfast table.

It was interesting that, in these last few weeks, Alma Stein would often look at Ruthie and tell her that she loved her and that she didn't know what she would ever do without her. To this Ruthie would always reply, "You will never have to find that out, Mother." Sometimes Alma would tell Ruthie the scrambled eggs tasted "extra special" that morning or that the coffee was "just perfect." It seemed that the two of them finally appreciated one another.

Ruthie enjoyed those precious moments but milking twice a day between twenty to twenty-five head of cattle, depending on how many cows were producing at any given time, as well as caring for her mother had physically exhausted Ruthie. The milking was not too tiring since her father had purchased the two new Surge milking machines shortly after Walter Junior died. It was possible to milk two cows at one time, as a harness attached to the cow held the milking machine in place. Whenever Ruthie felt tired doing the milking by herself, she drifted back to a time when all the cows were milked by hand, making the task truly laborious.

When she would go to church on Sunday with her mother, she heard others whispering about how tired Ruthie looked and that she seemed to be very gaunt. No doubt this accounted for why so many desserts and casseroles were taken to the Stein farmhouse, as the ladies of the church made sure to take to Alma and Ruthie over those weeks. While Ruthie knew the ladies of the church liked to gossip about one thing or another happening in their small community, they were also, for the most part, kind and charitable in helping their neighbors. Sometimes it almost seemed as if they competed with one another to see who would get to the Stein farmhouse first with a casserole, pie, or other baked good.

Ruthie had been very troubled about her mother's failing health and took her to a heart specialist in Watertown who their country doctor recommended. The doctor ordered an x-ray, which showed Alma had a very enlarged heart. He made it clear she would have to take it very easy and get as much rest as possible. He gave her mother something he referred to as "water pills" to take if her ankles and legs seemed swollen and some nitroglycerin to take if she had chest pains.

After seeing the specialist, Ruthie made sure to thoroughly clean and brighten the guest bedroom they had always maintained on the first floor just off the dining room. With Billy's help, she had moved her mother's bed to that room, and with Mrs. Packer's help she had moved all her mother's clothes to the guest room closet. The guest bedroom had an elongated window facing east, which allowed for a nice warming by the morning sun, along with a view of the barn and surrounding pastures. The downstairs bathroom was just off this bedroom. Alma would no longer have to climb stairs to go to bed at night. And Ruth wouldn't have to worry about her mother tumbling down them in the morning.

Despite her best efforts to make her mother more comfortable, Ruthie knew her mother wouldn't be around very much longer. She knew her father's death just eighteen months earlier had crushed her mother's spirit—that Alma Stein's reason for living had vanished. While her mother never seemed to tell her father how much she cared for him during his lifetime, the story she had told Ruthie the day of his burial contained the true measure of her love for Walter Senior. She missed holding his hand in bed at night.

She knew her father had loved his wife beyond measure and was always thankful to her for everything she did around the house, in the church, and for their neighbors. He always noticed a new fragrance she might have gotten from Avon or the new hat or dress she would purchase from time to time, complimenting her on how lovely she looked. Mother had been loved by an exceptional man, and now he was gone forever. Despite all the thoughts of being reunited in death, which Mother truly believed, the heaviness of his loss in this life was just too much for Alma Stein.

Chapter 3

February 1952 was one for the record books. If the groundhog was right, there would be six more weeks of winter. Ruthie prayed it would not prevent pickups and deliveries of their milk to the co-op, because every lost delivery meant lost cash flow the Steins badly needed. It took a real howling blizzard to keep the behemoth milk trucks from making their pickups and deliveries, but that did happen during some winters. Ruthie had helped her father dump their cans of milk onto the snow on more than one occasion when the milk truck from the cooperative could not make it through the famous blizzards of Upstate New York. Her father tried to take this milk dumping in stride, but Ruthie knew it bothered him greatly to waste such a large quantity of Holstein milk. Now, as Ruthie ran the farm and maintained the financial books for the humble enterprise, she understood even more how the loss of even one day's receipts could impact the farm's smooth operation.

She was lying in bed listening to the howling February snowstorm when she heard a faint scream from downstairs. She bounded out of bed and flew down the stairs from her second-story bedroom to find her mother lying in an awkward position on the cold, linoleum floor by her bed. Her mother was whimpering softly as Ruthie sat on the floor next to her, taking her mother's hand and inquiring if she hurt anywhere.

"Ruthie, I think I have broken something in my left leg or hip. I can't seem to move without horrible pain."

"You know I am strong enough to lift you into bed," Ruthie reassured her. "But I am not going to do that if you think you have broken something. I better get some help. Let me call the Packers and see if Billy and John can get over here, and I'll call Doc Ralph for his advice," Ruthie said breathlessly. Ruthie then got the pillow off the bed and put her mother's head gently on top while also covering her mother with the beautiful quilt Ruthie's grandmother had made for Alma as a wedding gift. She knew it was important to keep her mother as warm as possible, which was not an easy task at three in the morning before the wood furnace had been fired up for the morning chores.

She raced to the telephone to call the Packer residence. Thankfully, no one would be on the party line this time of day, so she would be able to reach the neighbors right away. It did seem like an eternity before Billy picked up the Packer phone with a somewhat grouchy tone, saying, "Who is this?"

Ruthie explained her predicament, and Billy's tone changed instantly. "That is terrible, Ruthie. Sure, I will be right there, and we will call Doc Ralph. Sounds like your mom needs to go to the hospital, and Doc should ride along, don't you think?"

"I agree, Billy, if we can rouse him at this early hour. And Lord knows, at seventy, he would be in no shape to navigate these snow-covered roads. Maybe you should fetch him first before you come here so he can advise us on how best to move Mom and give him a chance to wake up before he gets to the hospital. I know Mom must go to the hospital because she is moaning in such pain that it is certain she broke something, probably her hip," Ruthie answered.

"Well, we will call his home right now and tell him we are coming by, so he can advise us on what to do for your mother. We will call from Doc Ralph's when we leave with him. That way you'll know about when we will arrive at your house. Hang in there, Ruthie. Help is on the way," Billy said reassuringly.

By the time Billy had hung up the phone, his groggy parents and brother John were standing by the phone. "Sounds like real troubles at the Stein home," Mrs. Packer stated with a real measure of concern. "What has happened, Billy?"

"Ruthie says her mother fell out of bed and is on the floor moaning with pain. Ruthie thinks her mother has broken something, probably her hip, and any slight movement of Mrs. Stein just sends her into even more pain. She agrees with me we should try to rouse Doc Ralph and get him over to the Stein farmhouse as quickly as possible to advise us on how to move Alma, if he thinks she needs to get to the hospital in this raging snowstorm," Billy explained.

"Poor Alma. She has been rapidly failing since Walter died. She has had a bad heart for years, you know, and with Walter's death, it probably broke any heart she had left. You and John get dressed and go pick up Doc Ralph. Make sure you dress as warmly as possible because I doubt it is much above zero this morning. I'll call Doc now and tell him what has happened and ask if he will accompany you to the Steins and maybe the hospital if you are driving. I'll put some coffee on right now, so you can take a couple of thermoses with you to stay awake. Charles, why don't you start the car and warm it up for the boys? Don't forget to throw in a couple of shovels in case of any snow problems, and I'll give you a couple heavy quilts to put in the back seat," Bessie Packer directed.

Billy had to admit that his mother, although very annoying at times when ordering everybody about, was the most organized person he knew, possessing a steely disposition when a crisis arose.

———

Ruthie had raced back to her mother's side after throwing on her jeans, an undershirt, and a flannel shirt. She stoked up the furnace with plenty of wood and coal to warm up the house and told her mother that help was on the way. She took her mother's hand and asked if she was warm enough with the quilt and pillow protecting her from the cold linoleum floor.

Alma Stein gritted her teeth and nodded her head in the affirmative. Ruthie began to feel some warmth coming through the floor register nearby the bed.

"Ruthie," Alma Stein pleaded, "please don't let them take me to the hospital just to die. This may be my time to join your father, Ruthie, and I'd rather die right here in my own bed I shared with your father for forty years."

"Mother, I promise if they do take you to the hospital to fix a broken bone, I will get you home to this bed. Don't you think I would want you right here with me? And stop talking about death, Mother. Remember what it says in the Bible. Only the Lord knows the date and time he will come for us."

Alma Stein tried to smile, but her pain was so intense she could only look at her dutiful daughter and whisper, "My dear Ruthie, you need to be realistic. I haven't felt well for several months, and I have a feeling this tumble out of bed is a signal the Lord is coming for me. I know you will do what is best for me. We haven't been the closest, and that is my fault, Ruthie. I want you to know that I would not want any other person but you with me right now because you are the most honest and loving person I have ever known. I am sorry I haven't said that before, but always remember I said it now. In some ways, I have always been a little bit jealous of you and your big heart and how close you and your father seemed to be—how he beamed with pride when you were with him at church or anywhere for that matter."

Alma was out of breath by the time she finished her last sentence and tried to rest her head quietly on the pillow. Ruthie was wiping away tears from her eyes, wondering if she'd lose her mother before help arrived. She looked at the alarm clock in her mother's room. It was now 3:35 a.m. Surely Billy would arrive soon with the doc, but by the sound of the vicious winds outside the farmhouse, she knew the drive was treacherous and she tried to be patient.

It was just about twenty minutes later when she heard her downstairs door burst open and listened as the familiar gait of Billy resounded across the wooden floor downstairs.

"Ruthie, we are here. We made it and Doc Ralph too," Billy shouted. As he looked through the doorway of Alma Stein's bedroom, he saw the sad scene of her twisted body on the floor and Ruthie sitting Indian style next to her.

Billy waited patiently as Doc Ralph slowly walked across the kitchen and dining room into Alma's new downstairs bedroom. "My dear Alma," Doc said quietly as he leaned down to the floor and gently touched her. "Looks like you had quite a tumble here. How did it happen, do you remember?"

"All I can really remember is feeling like I needed to use the bathroom, and the next thing I remember is being on this cold, cold floor and yelling out for Ruthie," Alma stated, whispering in obvious pain.

"Well, let's get you off that freezing floor right away. Let me move your neck if I can, Alma." As Doc slowly palpated Alma's neck he asked Alma if it hurt, and she weakly responded, "No."

Doc turned to Billy and John and instructed them to very gently move Alma back up on her bed. He then continued his examination. Alma screamed out in pain when Doc moved her left leg and hip.

Doc stepped back from the bed and told Alma he was sure she had broken her hip and perhaps her pelvis. Alma needed to go to the hospital for some emergency treatment.

"But what treatment would that be, Doc? There isn't much they could do for an old woman like me if that's the truth of the situation. I might just as well stay right here in my bed and die at home," Alma pleaded.

"Well I understand your thinking, Alma. I really do. But we need to get you to the hospital for an x-ray to confirm my diagnosis. I might be wrong. I'm not a bone doc. And if I am right, they can get you warmed up, make sure you don't have any other physical problems, and send you back home with some pain medications to get you through the next few weeks. I don't think it is quite time for you to exit this earth. So, let's get you to the hospital. Don't you think that would be a good idea, Ruthie?" Doc Ralph sought affirmation of his plan.

"Of course, Doc. I agree completely. We need that x-ray. Things might not be as bad as Mother believes them to be, and Lord knows she will need some medication for her pain whatever is wrong. But should we wait for first light with that storm blowing outside?" Ruthie inquired with a measure of concern.

"I won't say the trip will be easy, but John did an excellent job driving me over here, and if the weatherman on the radio is right, this is just the beginning of a good blow, which could last three or four days. We wait any longer, and we can't be sure we can get your mom over there for days," Doc reasoned.

"Very well then," Ruthie responded. "I'll get lots of warm blankets and quilts to keep her covered. John, could you get that car started again to warm it up?" Ruthie inquired.

John was out the front door into the continuing blizzard in a flash. He had his doubts about the trip to the hospital, but this was where his unusually fine driving skills could be put to good use. He had won every tractor-pulling contest he had entered in Future Farmers of America and had a shelf of small trophies to prove it.

Billy helped Ruthie gather the needed coverings for Alma as Doc used his stethoscope to check on Alma's heart. While fetching the quilts and blankets in Alma's room, Billy spied an old, narrow closet door leaning against the wall. He returned to Alma Stein's room and asked Doc if they could cover the top of the door with a couple blankets, place Alma on top, and keep her prone as they carefully moved her to the car. Then they could carry her to the back seat of the car and slowly pull the blankets under her onto the seat.

"Excellent suggestion, son," Doc responded.

The movement of Alma from her bed to the back seat of the car went smoothly, considering the snow-draped front steps of the farmhouse and the big flakes of snow that continued to drift down ceaselessly. Ruthie climbed into the back seat and helped Billy and Johnny settle her mom on the seat next to her by sliding Alma off the makeshift livery with the blankets sliding easily across the bench seat. Alma's head rested on Ruthie's lap. The three men crawled into the front and crept out of the driveway onto the almost indistinguishable roadway. The windshield wipers could barely keep up with the falling snow, and John had to drive a lot from his memory of going over this road hundreds of times before. The compartment was silent except for an occasional moan from Alma when the car went over a bump or seemed to slip sideways for a moment. Ruthie stroked her mother's hair and kept telling her John was doing a great job driving and that they would be at the hospital soon.

Ruthie prayed silently, *Lord somehow get us all there safely, please. Let Mother live.*

It seemed an eternity, but John was soon pulling up to the emergency exit of the hospital. True to form, Bessie Packer had phoned ahead and let the hospital know they would be arriving with Mrs. Stein, who had likely broken a hip. An orderly and nurse were waiting at the emergency door, and with the help of Billy and John, they got Mrs. Stein hoisted onto a gurney and into the examining room. Ruthie could hear Doc Ralph tell the hospital personnel what he suggested were Mrs. Stein's injuries. He admitted that an orthopedic consult would surely be needed after an x-ray and physical examination of Alma had taken place. The nurse offered the suggestion that Doc Ralph could go ahead and authorize the x-ray since he had hospital privileges there, and when Dr. Carter made his rounds in a couple hours, he could examine the x-ray. The nurse further explained that doing the x-ray now would mean they could get Alma settled in a hospital bed more quickly and give her some sedation for pain.

Doc told the nurse it all seemed very logical and that he and the others would go to the waiting room to warm up and get some coffee. The nurse assured them coffee and doughnuts would be available in the hospital cafeteria now, as it always opened by 5:00 a.m. to start breakfast for all the patients. She would call the cafeteria and explain someone would be down for coffee. The orderly and nurse pushed Alma's gurney to the x-ray room door and disappeared.

Chapter 4

Billy and John headed off to the cafeteria after escorting Doc Ralph and Ruthie into the waiting room. That way, they would be close by in case Dr. Carter, the bone doc, came to the hospital earlier than expected. After Ruthie sat down, she glanced over at Doc Ralph and saw how haggard he appeared. "I am so sorry to drag you out on a night like this," Ruthie apologized.

Doc Ralph smiled at Ruthie and cleared his throat before speaking. "No apologies needed, my dear. It's my job and a pleasure to do for your family. You know, Ruthie, on the way over here tonight, I was thinking how your father was responsible for getting me to our little burg of Four Corners. He got me set up in our comfortable house, which was big enough for my office and a waiting room. I was told by Mrs. Packer that your dad got up in front of the Methodist Church one Sunday in January 1920 and said it was time Four Corners had a doctor. It was essential that people did not have to drive to Watertown all the time for medical attention, especially when someone was injured on the farm, got pneumonia, or was expecting a baby. He apparently suggested the community pull together out of Christian charity and collect money for a down payment on a house to get a new doctor he knew about from Cornell to come here. He mentioned that Methodists always provided their pastors with parsonages to complement their small salaries, so the souls of the community were healed. Now, it was time to think about doing the same for someone who could heal bodies."

Doc Ralph continued, "Within two months on a blustery March first night like this one, I raced to your farmhouse to deliver you. I was scared to death, not of the roads, but because I was a new doctor who had never delivered a baby all on my own before. Oh, I had attended deliveries in medical school and my year of internship at the hospital, but the thought of delivering you all by myself on your parents' kitchen table was downright frightening. But you know who got me through it? Your dad helped with the delivery as tears streamed down his face. All the time he was saying, 'Yes, Doc. That's right. I can see the baby's head. You're doing great, Doc. Thank God for you, Doc.' He got me all convinced of my brilliance, and driving home that night, I felt real joy about bringing you into the world and realized it wasn't my brilliance but your Dad's confidence in me, with his years of experience delivering heifers and bulls, that made the process seem natural and good. I remember him shouting out as I held you up, 'Daddy's little girl is here. Oh, thank you, God, thank you, Doc.' I suppose you understand you were daddy's little girl who grew up to be a strong, bright woman he adored because you shared his love of the Stein farm," Doc concluded.

Tears crept down Ruthie's cheeks. "Thanks for that story, Doc. I'd never heard it before. I miss my father so much," Ruthie whispered, choking back more tears.

"I can understand that, Ruthie. Your father admired your mind and caring disposition so much. He often told me he wished he had the money to send you to vet school at Cornell. He knew you were so bright and so good with the animals on your farm. He also knew your mother wanted a more traditional female vocation for you so, even if he'd had the money, your mother would have thought it a waste to spend it on a college education for a young woman," Doc Ralph said as he stared at the hospital floor.

Soon Billy and John were back from the cafeteria with doughnuts and coffee. All watched as John devoured two doughnuts in about one minute. Ruthie observed Billy glaring at his brother as if to say,

"How can you think about your stomach at a time like this?" Ruthie understood John's hunger. Ordinarily, this was about the time the Packers would be heading to the farmhouse for a big breakfast. She reached for a doughnut, took a bite, and said, "Tastes like these were just fried, John. Glad you got a few, and you eat as many as you can. After all, I expect you will be taking us back home in this dreadful storm, and the good Lord only knows how that will go. It might be a good while before we see food again."

John smiled back at Ruthie and glared back at his brother. Ruthie was always a woman of few words, but when she did speak, it was always in a manner to calm and soothe. John did understand why his brother liked Ruthie. Even if she was rather plain-looking, her gentle personality made her seem like an angel at times. He knew he would never be attracted to her romantically, but he had always wished she was his sister. From what he had heard, Walter Junior wasn't always kind to Ruthie in their school years. But once Walter Junior died on Omaha Beach, the focus had always been on his heroism, rather than Ruthie's infinite kindness.

About an hour had gone by when Dr. Carter stepped into the waiting room. "Hi, folks. Ruthie, your mother has suffered a broken left hip. I am afraid there is not much we can do about it. Her heart is very weak, and hip pinning is out of the question. All we can do is keep her as comfortable as possible in here for a few days with sedation, and then I'd recommend you transfer her to that new convalescent home over on Pratt Street. She is not going to be able to do the smallest things for herself, and with you running that farm, I just can't see you taking care of her too. I know it is expensive, but maybe there would be some of that new federal funding available. You'd have to ask them how much it would be per month. Truthfully, we know it is just a matter of a few months, even weeks, before your mom is gone," Dr. Carter sadly commented.

"I appreciate your concern, Dr. Carter," Ruthie replied, "but Mom is going home. She wants to be home, and home she will go. She will end her days with dignity in her own bed. I can manage somehow. That is what we Steins do."

Billy was worried about Dr. Carter's warnings. His dear friend, Ruthie, was amazing, but he knew Dr. Carter was right. Ruthie was biting off more than she could chew for sure. He had been thinking about this for a few hours as they rode to the hospital, sat in the waiting room, and discussed Doc Ralph's very probable diagnosis. Billy spoke up immediately. "Ruthie, could I talk to you outside for a minute, please?" he asked.

Ruthie stepped outside the hospital waiting room with Billy and could see the concerned look on his face. "Look, Billy," she challenged, "I know what you are going to say before you say it. Mom is coming home with me. That's all there is to it."

Billy was not offended by Ruthie's abrupt words and smiled. He knew Ruthie stubbornly responded this way when she was convinced her way was best, and it usually was. "Ruthie, I know you are a very smart woman, but now you've become a mind reader too? I am not here to question your decision to take your mother home, but to suggest a way you can have your mom home with some help."

Ruthie sighed deeply, knowing she had been too sharp with Billy. But while she would soften responses to him, she was not going to accept additional help from the Packer family. She faced him with arms crossed but smiled. "What is your idea?"

Billy continued his conversation. "While I've been sitting in this waiting room trying to figure out how you could continue your farm tasks and take care of your mother, it suddenly occurred to me that there was someone who would fit the bill perfectly to take care of your mother and household chores. I believe a couple years ago you met my cousin Ruth Packer, who came to our home to visit for a week during haying season? She was such a great help to my mother in cooking meals for the extra hired hands. If my memory doesn't fail me, she might have made a pie or two for you?"

It didn't take any effort for Ruthie to remember Ruth. She clearly remembered meeting this warm, engaging woman, and she had thought then, *it's too bad she doesn't live closer than Cooperstown. We could be great friends.* Ruth was about five feet four with blue eyes and the thickest dark brown hair Ruthie had ever seen. But of greater note to Ruthie was the constant twinkle in Ruth's eye and a quick wit that filled Ruthie with joy.

"Yes, I remember her, Billy," Ruthie replied. What does this have to do with my mother's situation?"

"Well, Billy replied, "It just so happens that both her parents are gone now. She is single, and as you may or may not remember, she taught high school English at the Cooperstown High School, filling in for a man who was recovering from his Korean War wounds. He came back to work in January, and now she's looking for another job. She rents a room in Cooperstown and lives off her meager savings. It seems that, when her father died, she learned he had mortgaged the family home to send her to Smith College. While she was teaching, and with the help of her mother's social security, she could make the mortgage payment. But then her mother died, and she lost her job a month later. I truly believe she would welcome a free place to live in exchange for taking care of your mother until perhaps another teaching position comes her way. She took care of her own parents and did a superb job. Maybe you could give her a hundred dollars a month for her personal needs?"

Ruthie thought for a moment and had a few more questions for Billy. "Ruth was most friendly, and if she is your cousin, I have no questions about her integrity. And yes, she made me two of the most delicious apple pies I have ever eaten, which also includes my Grandmother Stein's county fair award-winning apple pies. But why would she want to come here to live on a farm with me and take care of Mother when she is a teacher? Seems like pretty boring work for a Smith graduate," Ruthie pointed out.

Billy knew his response had to be convincing but not pushy. He recalled how his cousin Ruth was most amazed at the thought of

Ruthie running a farm by herself after her father had died. She had asked him many questions about Ruthie Stein and the whole family clan. He had explained how he had tried to get Ruthie to marry him on more than one occasion. His cousin Ruth had said, "That is a real shame, Billy. I can see what a catch she would be for you." Billy had noted at the time that, besides his mother, who desired a Stein-Packer farm enterprise, no one had seen the sense in his desire to marry Ruthie. He had later thought about his cousin's comments and assessed Ruth was quite enamored with Ruthie. He knew Ruthie would like Ruth as well because of her unusual college education, not something their community often saw among women. Given Ruthie's own fine mind, he just knew conversation between them would be continuous and easy.

Billy wanted to make certain Ruthie didn't believe it was a done deal and let her mind warm to the possibility. "Now understand, Ruthie, this is just my idea. Maybe you are right that Ruth would not want to live on a farm. But as I said, she did take care of both her parents, and she told me after her mother's funeral that taking care of her parents was the finest thing she had ever done and would never regret it. Should I ask her if this is something she'd consider, and are these proposed terms acceptable?" Billy inquired.

"I think your idea is a good one. Go ahead and ask her," Ruthie replied. "I can manage finding an extra hundred dollars somewhere in the farm budget."

Chapter 5

Ruth had been taking care of Mrs. Stein for about two months now, and Ruthie could not have been happier. Every night after evening chores and in the mornings after the milking, Ruthie would walk into a kitchen that smelled even more wonderful than her mother's kitchen when she had awoken to the enticing smell of baked goods as a young girl. Hot coffee was on the table, and two places had been set for her and Ruth. Ruth bathed her mother regularly and always had her in fresh laundered clothes, also taking a tray three times a day into her mother's room for meals. Her mother slept most of the time these days and was in what the doctors called congestive heart failure. When Ruthie went into her mother's room, her mother often called her Ruth, instead of Ruthie. Perhaps this was normal, given their names were nearly the same. However, somehow Ruthie knew the woman taking care of her household and mother now was not a version of herself but an insightful, brilliant, and very feminine woman who talked to her so sweetly each day at mealtimes and around the fireplace at night.

Both women had their bedrooms on the second floor of the drafty farmhouse, but Ruthie noted that Ruth could often be found in the mornings sound asleep on the daybed in the dining room her father had once used while taking naps after morning chores and breakfast. She suspected that her mother sometimes called out for Ruth during the night, and Ruth wanted to be closer to mother's bedroom. She would look at Ruth as she slept peacefully on the daybed and would sometimes make certain Ruth had a blanket or two pulled up to the chin before going down to the basement and firing up the furnace. She didn't realize that Ruth was sometimes pretending to be asleep when this happened. And when Ruthie left the room, Ruth would smile to herself thinking about how Ruthie was demonstrating her care for her.

As Ruthie stoked the furnace, she would think about her lovely new friend lying peacefully upstairs. She thought about how, after breakfast and milking each day, Ruth would insist Ruthie lie down on the same daybed for a quick nap before resuming any barn chores. As Ruthie would lie on the bed, she would inhale from the pillow that sweet fragrance of lavender Ruth always seemed to have. It was then that Ruthie would pray, "God, thank you for bringing one of your angels into my house to help me when I thought I could never go on."

Alma Stein, due to Ruth's excellent care, lived on and seemed to enjoy all the attention from Ruth, always remembering to thank Ruth for her kindnesses. In the early afternoons when Mrs. Stein was awake, Ruth would read to Mrs. Stein from one of the many books she had brought with her to the farmhouse. When the postal service delivered *Look* magazine, Ruth made sure to read it for Alma from cover to cover. At night, after dinner, Ruth would go over the articles in the *Watertown Daily Times* with Mrs. Stein as Alma fell asleep.

———

May 1952

She had listened to the coughing for too long. Every time she heard that cough, which sounded as if Ruth would cough up her lungs, Ruthie winced. She had to do something. She remembered her mother had kept a vaporizer in the pantry. Ruthie didn't even wait to find her slippers, dashing across the cold linoleum floor to the stairs. She made short work of descending the stairs and secured the vaporizer. On the way back upstairs, Ruthie remembered that Vicks VapoRub and a hot towel could also break up congestion. There was some old Vicks in the upstairs medicine cabinet. She also discovered a full box of Smith Brothers cough drops.

Ruthie filled the vaporizer with water and ran hot water on a washcloth. She juggled all these items as she hurried to Ruth's room. Ruth was still coughing continuously. Ruthie set the vaporizer on the floor and knocked gently on the door. "Ruth, may I come in?" she inquired.

"You never need to ask that question," Ruth replied. "My dear Ruthie, has my coughing kept you awake? Golly, what time is it? Don't you have to get up soon to do the milking? I'll try to stop this infernal coughing, so you can get a couple hours more sleep. No need to worry about me, Ruthie. Go back to sleep," Ruth directed.

As Ruthie entered the room, she realized just how cold Ruth's room had become. "My goodness, Ruth, it is freezing in here! Why haven't you told me how cold it gets in here at night? As soon as I am done here I am going to stoke up the furnace with more coal and wood," Ruthie assured her very sick friend.

"What's all this you are bringing to me?" Ruth inquired.

"Just some items Mother found helpful for me and Walter Junior when we got horrible colds. First, I don't want to embarrass you in any way, Ruth, but we need to rub this Vick's on your chest right away, so I can put this hot cloth on top of your chest. Do you want me to rub it on, or would you prefer to do it yourself?" Ruthie asked.

"Well I don't mind at all if you do that, Ruthie. You are apparently the doctor on duty tonight," Ruth responded with a smile.

"Okay then, Ruth, here I go." Ruthie first propped Ruth up in the bed, reminding her it would be much better for her to be elevated so she could breathe easier. Ruthie then gently untied the top of Ruth's flannel nightgown and pushed it down to Ruth's shoulders blades so only the upper chest was exposed. Ruthie rubbed her hands together vigorously, so they wouldn't be stone cold when she applied the Vicks

VapoRub. Opening the jar, Ruthie reached in for a large glob and began to gently rub the substance onto Ruth's chest.

"This will hopefully break up some of the congestion," Ruthie reassured as she continued to apply VapoRub.

"Can't say the smell of this stuff has gotten any better since the time my father used it himself, but that gentle message is comforting. No one has ever taken care of me like this, Ruthie. Thanks." Ruth smiled.

"Well, I am not nearly done yet," Ruthie said with emphasis. "You're going to feel so much better when this washcloth is applied." With that, she carefully laid the now lukewarm washcloth on Ruth's chest.

"Oh yes, that is better," Ruth replied. I can feel that Vicks being absorbed into my skin, and it feels so soothing." Ruth relaxed into the three pillows Ruthie had put behind her.

Ruth got an old maple chair, put a towel on the seat, and set up the vaporizer. After it was plugged in, within short order, it was expelling a fine mist in the air, funneled toward Ruth. "Don't you think I should call Doc Ralph in the morning and see if he can get by to check on you and make sure you don't have pneumonia or something?" Ruthie suggested.

"Oh no, heaven's no," Ruth stated emphatically. "That's too costly and unnecessary. I am sure, if I have just a couple more hours of sleep, I can get up and fix your Mom's breakfast as well as ours," Ruth said.

"There is absolutely no way I will let you do that, Ruth. You are too sick. If you won't stay in bed for yourself, then stay in bed for Mother. She doesn't need that cold, and I am perfectly capable of making scrambled eggs and toast when I get in from the barn, as well as brewing a steaming pot of tea for all of us," Ruthie stated firmly.

Ruthie didn't quite know where her demanding demeanor had come from and apologized for sounding so bossy. "I'm so worried about you. I am sure I sounded a little heavy-handed. Let me assure you that you are not the first patient I have attended, but I have to say you are my favorite," Ruthie said as she pulled the quilt up over Ruth's shoulders and handed her the box of Smith Brothers cough drops. "Sweet dreams, my friend," Ruthie said as she quietly retreated from the bedroom.

Chapter 6

July 1952

It was a very hot Sunday in the Methodist church, even with the windows open and a slight breeze blowing into the sanctuary. Ruth had joined Ruthie in the church pew every Sunday since she'd moved into the Stein home. Alma Stein insisted Ruth leave her side for Sunday services because Ruth "needs to get away for a few hours at least." Everyone in the church had come to love Ruth. She was very friendly, had the most beautiful smile, and was by far the best-dressed woman in the church. Ruthie tried to hide the pride she felt for having Ruth in her life and sitting next to her in church.

Ruthie recalled how Ruth, just one month into her church attendance, filled in for their ill church pianist. The pastor asked if anyone could play the piano for their service since the regular pianist, Virginia Oppenheimer, was home very sick from a bad cold. After a few seconds of uncomfortable silence, Ruth stood up and said, "I'll give it a try, Reverend, but I might be a little rusty." The Reverend gave Ruth a broad smile and said, "Well, whatever you do on the piano will probably be twice as good as our singing, Miss Packer. We are not the heavenly choir," he added with a chuckle.

Ruthie was in a state of shock as she watched Ruth move to the piano bench. She had no idea Ruth played the piano. It had never been mentioned, probably because there was no piano in the Stein home. The first hymn to be played was "Are Ye Able," and Ruth told the fifty souls gathered that she would practice by playing through the hymn once and then they would all sing together the second time around. Like most of Ruth's endeavors her piano playing was exceptional, and Ruthie watched as the people around her smiled with appreciation. Ruth's skillful fingers flew across the keys. Ruthie caught a glimpse of Billy smiling at his cousin and then smiling at her, nodding his head in approval of his cousin's talents.

The congregation responded to her spirited playing by singing more robustly than ever before. After the last stanza, Ruth came and sat next to Ruthie, so she could listen to the sermon. Ruthie patted her gently on the shoulder as if to say, "Well done," as did the lady sitting on the other side of Ruth. After the sermon, Ruth played the second hymn, and during the collection, Ruth played from memory "Count Your Blessings" with the flair of a Gospel pianist. More heads turned in disbelief, as she seemed to get sounds out of the old piano they had never heard before.

As the parishioners left the church, most of them made sure to shake Ruth's hand or give her a hug of thanks. Ruthie stood just outside the door of the church, still stunned at Ruth's hidden talent. She wondered what Virginia Oppenheimer would say when she heard about her substitute. As Ruth was shaking the parson's hand and hearing his effusive praise, she heard Ruth reply, "Well, Reverend, no one plays the piano as well as Virginia, and if I had never heard those hymns before, I would have been in trouble."

After they got in the car and had headed down the road, Ruthie commented, "That was a pretty good job for someone who just happened to know these hymns! When they say someone is well-rounded, I guess that would be you."

"Well I am pretty well-rounded as anyone can see," she patted her little stomach and laughed. "Truth be told, I was a pretty spoiled young lady. Mother thought a proper education for a young woman included piano lessons. I took them for eight years and played for recitals at Cooperstown High. I even thought about being a music teacher, but English was my favorite subject, so I majored in that at Smith. There were lots of pianos at Smith, so I would go and play to relax, usually Chopin," Ruth explained.

"I feel badly that we have no piano in the house," Ruthie sighed.

"Oh, that's just fine, Ruthie. I have plenty to keep me busy these days, and I expect that after today, no one would mind if I practiced on the church piano every now and then."

"Mind! After today's performance, the church will probably ask you to put on a recital for the whole community and sell tickets for the church treasury." Ruthie laughed. "But don't you think I would like to sit in our living room and listen to you play just for me?" Ruthie pleaded. "I am definitely going to get you a piano. Just you wait and see."

"Well," Ruth began, "I would never play the piano for you unless you agreed to sing along when you felt like exercising those perfect-pitch pipes you have. I have neglected to tell you what a beautiful singing voice you have. Have you ever considered joining the choir?"

"I sang for the congregation quite a bit when I was little, starting at about age five. My father seemed so proud to hear me belt out those John and Charles Wesley songs from memory. After I got into my high school years, I was so busy with homework and farm chores, I let the singing lapse," Ruthie explained.

Little did the congregation know that Sunday as all listened to Ruth's debut that one year later, Virginia Oppenheimer would tell the pastor that her arthritic fingers would no longer allow her to play the piano for the church. There would be no question who would be doing that job. It was Ruth.

When they got home, Ruthie could smell the beef roast Ruth had popped into the oven before they left for church. Replete with baked potatoes and some canned string beans Ruth warmed up on top of the stove, the two friends sat down at the table, said a blessing as they held hands, and began the Sunday dinner. The slow cooked beef didn't even need a knife, and there was some delicious bread and applesauce to accompany the main fare. Dessert was a piece of Ruth's German chocolate cake.

Chapter 7

August 22, 1952

Billy Packer was delighted the arrangement with Ruth had worked out. However, he knew Alma Stein was not long for this world, and he had one last chance to convince Ruthie she should marry him. His mother had advised him that, once Alma Stein had passed on, Ruth would no longer have a purpose at the Stein farm; she doubted Ruthie would keep her on once the caretaking responsibilities of Mrs. Stein were done. A summer fish fry was scheduled for the coming Saturday night, and his mother suggested he invite Ruthie to go with him. He did not delay in asking and made sure Ruth was around in the Stein kitchen when he did.

"I am not sure I should go, Billy," Ruthie replied. "Mom is in a most weakened condition. I can't leave Ruth here all alone to deal with that. What if Mom passes away while I am out having this great time with you? I'd never forgive myself," Ruthie answered with sincere reservation in her voice.

Ruth quickly spoke up. "Ruthie, it would do you good to get out for once. I'll be just fine, and you know I can call the fire station telephone if there is an emergency. Go, go, and have a great time dancing and eating that delicious fish."

Ruthie felt bewildered and trapped. The last thing she wanted to do was to go to that fish fry with Billy. She much preferred settling into one of the Saturday nights the two ladies had come to enjoy. Both would have a special meal and then take turns with a hot bath. They would put on housecoats and listen to music on the radio, as well as discuss all the things going on in the community and at church. Often, Ruth would tell Ruthie about her days at Smith College, and sometimes she'd read a poem or two she had acquired in her English textbooks from Smith. Ruth's voice was so soothing it often put Ruthie to sleep. Ruth would usually get up and gently move Ruthie's hundred-year-old rocking chair just enough to awaken Ruthie to say it was time for bed. This was the Saturday night Ruthie thought was ideal, not socializing with other women who often competed for male attention at these community functions. She was also disappointed Ruth was so eager to send her off on this date with her cousin. She had thought that Ruth had become a fast friend who wouldn't mind living with her on a permanent basis.

"Well, how can I say no when two Packers are ganging up on me," Ruthie said with some hesitation.

Billy couldn't believe Ruthie had said yes, and Ruth quietly walked back into Mrs. Stein's bedroom.

Ruthie was very uncomfortable at the Volunteer Fire Department's annual fish fry and dance. She didn't even know how to dance properly. Apart from a few lessons in high school music class, dancing was never her priority. "Look, Ruthie," Billy pleaded, "it has been six months since your mother took ill, and everyone will be wanting to see you. Except for church each Sunday, you don't go anywhere and do anything."

Billy saw the sad expression on Ruthie's face and immediately felt responsible for a well-meaning conversation gone wrong. "Oh, Ruthie, I would never expect you to invite me over for a meal as busy as you are with those twenty head of milking cows. I was trying to say everyone's missed seeing you at community events like this. I've missed seeing you except for a quick hug you let me give you each week after church. It is so hard for me to think of the kindest woman in this farm community having to be all alone in that big farmhouse, the only surviving member of her family."

"You've always been so wonderful in looking out for me," Ruthie conceded. "But you know, I really don't feel all that lonely with all those animals that need me and Ruth, who has been such a help with mother. And my young collie, Jenny, is always by my side. She's so smart she even knows how to go to you for help. You remember how I had gotten the tractor overturned in the back fields and I sent her to your barn barking for help."

"I certainly do remember that day," Billy replied. "I was so worried you had really hurt yourself. I knew what Jenny wanted immediately and started following her on foot as fast as I could. When I first saw that tractor from a distance, I thought, *Oh my God. Ruthie must be trapped under that old piece of junk.* And I started running even faster than I thought I could. It was lucky you didn't die that day. There was an angel on your shoulder, Ruthie, and it was all the evidence I needed to try to convince you I should be in your life as more than just a friend. Someone needs to be with you on that farm, and that someone should be me."

"Well, that may be your interpretation, Billy, but what I was try-ing to say is that I don't feel unsafe or insecure with Ruth and Jenny around and good neighbors like you less than a mile away," Ruthie said.

Ruthie knew Billy liked her a lot and had hinted about getting married. She always steered clear of those conversations, if she could, with one or more excuses. Nothing seemed to work with Billy. She couldn't understand why he liked her "in that way" so much. When she looked in the mirror, she saw a "plain-Jane" farm girl with no makeup, short-cropped hair, a little overweight. She tried as best as she could to conform to the social norms of wearing dresses on occasions such as this one and every week at church. But if she had her way, she would never get out of her overalls except to sleep and to have them laundered.

Fortunately, she did know how to wash clothes properly and hang them out on the line, and she was always impeccable about her bathing. In fact, since Ruth had arrived in the home, she had even bathed in some lavender-smelling bubble bath she had been given by Ruth. Soaking in a tub every Saturday evening after one of Ruth's delicious meals had become a true luxury for her. The hot water soothed her sore muscles, relaxing her more than anything else. She had even installed a radio in the bathroom, turned to the only local station, which played popular music. Jenny would lie down on the rug by the tub, wag her tail, and look up at Ruthie as Ruthie's cheery voice sang along to some of the songs.

While it was obvious her canine liked her dinnertime after the farm chores were done for the day, when Ruthie would give her some scraps from her plate, all Ruthie had to say to her companion was, "Bath?" and Jenny would tear up the stairs to the bathroom and lie down on her rug with her tail wagging frantically. Ruth and Ruthie never failed to chuckle at her dog's predictability. There was something wonderful about this predictable behavior. Was it that Jenny just loved company so much or that she regarded bath time as a very special time of the day with nice smells and soothing sounds from the radio? Wasn't it amazing Jenny asked for so little in life? There would be no way she could disappoint this companion, for all Jenny wanted was some food and some love. That was something Ruthie could always give her. Human beings were so much more demanding, except for Ruth, who had slipped into her life and her heart so effortlessly.

After wandering about in her thoughts, her mind returned to Billy, who was waiting for a response. "Billy, what do you find in me that is attractive to you? I can't figure that out for the life of me. Cindy Adams is always flirting with you at church and forever bringing you pies at your farm. Now, she's a very attractive woman with obviously excellent cooking skills. You are lucky she is still single at twenty-five. Here I am at thirty-two, just an old farm girl who really doesn't want to be anything else than that," Ruthie stated emphatically.

"I would not want you to be anything different if you married me," Billy replied forcefully. "You are attractive to me and so physically fit, all a farm wife should be. Of course, Cindy is probably every man's dream, and why she isn't married yet is a mystery. But, Ruthie, don't you realize how wonderful you are? I am not talking about outside, Ruthie. I am talking about inside. That gigantic heart of yours surely needs someone to return all the love and care you give so effortlessly. Then there is that very sharp mind of yours, which you constantly deny. Have you forgotten you were the top student in our high school, in fact throughout every grade? You should have gone to college like my cousin, Ruth, if your parents had encouraged you more. And I am glad they didn't because you are still here. I am proud of how you've succeeded with the Stein farm since your father died," Billy said.

Billy continued his campaign to get Ruthie to at least agree to a formal courtship. "You see, Ruthie, I have always taken to you. And as much as you think you are unattractive, I beg to differ. Those long eyelashes over those lovely hazel eyes hooked me in a long time ago. It's a good thing to want an intelligent, kind, steady, and faithful wife who knows a lot about farming. And heaven knows I don't care if you can't cook. We could do everything together on a farm, even the cooking."

"Well my goodness, Billy, where'd you get those thoughts on marriage? Doesn't sound like any of the men I know about in these parts." Ruthie laughed.

"Think about it, Ruthie. How many married couples around here are truly happy? You know, and I know, that my own parents aren't happy with one another anymore. They have fallen into this silence with one another. When they do talk to one another, it is always about something practical, and they usually end up in a fight. Sure, my mom was very attractive when they met, and Pop could charm bees out of a hive and not get stung.

"All that changed after we kids got to be adolescents. It is almost like they gave up trying to make each other just a little happier. It would never be like that with us, Ruthie. I just know that instinctively. I want a woman in life who enjoys the things I enjoy, which is mostly all about farming—the change of seasons, the animals, the smell of the fresh soil being tilled in the spring, those busy summer days that are nevertheless filled with big meals to keep up our energy and tasty lemonade. I know you well enough, Ruthie, that I can say you like all those things too. Won't you agree to take my hand and grow old together on these two farms? At least give me an engagement period with you. After six months, if you can't see this same future, I'll stop my campaign for marriage and end the engagement gracefully, so we are still good friends. I'll never complain to you about turning down my offer," Billy pleaded.

Ruthie was so moved by Billy's words she started to tear up. "Billy, you are surely the kindest man I have ever met and the only man, save my father, who has ever complimented me on anything other than my academics in high school and my knowledge of farming. But becoming your wife would seem so unnatural to me because all my life I have thought of you as the kind, thoughtful brother I never had. We played together every day as small children and ate our lunches together at school. It is not that I don't love you. I really do. But I love you as a brother, and I doubt I will ever get married. I think, if we tried marriage, we would end up like your folks and all the other couples who drop into silence after years together. I don't want to lose the best friend I have ever had by becoming your wife. Can you understand that?" Ruthie inquired.

"I was afraid you would say that," Billy answered with a downcast look. "But if you ever change your mind, let me know because the offer still stands."

"It is time you got married, Billy Packer, and I suggest you go over and start talking to Cindy Adams, who has been staring at you all evening and surely wondering why you are spending so much time with me when you could be dancing with her," Ruthie advised.

"Well, I will ask her for one dance. However, it is you that I will take home tonight. My mother would never approve of ditching you in favor of a drive home with Cindy Adams." Billy smiled as he turned toward Cindy and the women Cindy had been furiously chatting with since she had arrived at the fish fry.

Ruthie watched as Billy did a credible job of swirling Cindy about the floor to that new song, "It Had to Be You." Cindy beamed from the moment she took Billy's hand until the song ended and Billy had gotten Cindy some punch. Ruthie was happy Billy had listened to her and she was glad the conversation about marriage was finally spoken and over. She did love Billy very much, just as she had told him. But she did not imagine them sleeping next to each other every night or having children together. She knew Billy's mother encouraged him to court her but with ulterior motives. The Packer farm and the Stein farm would make a very effective enterprise if joined together through their marriage. She knew Billy well enough to know his motives for wanting to marry her were pure, and she felt badly about letting him down. But in the long haul, she knew she was doing him a favor by not subjecting him to the tension that would always occur between his mother and Ruthie as Mrs. Packer tried to direct the affairs of both her son and daughter-in-law.

Chapter 8

Ruth did not hear Ruthie return from the fish fry and had gone to bed after tending to Mrs. Stein. She found herself crying when she thought about losing Ruthie from her life. She knew she was in love with her, but how could they ever be together? Where was God in all her confusion? She uttered out loud, "Dear God, why have you brought me to this place to fall in love with this woman?"

Almost immediately, she heard a light knock on her door and Ruthie's very concerned inquiry if everything was all right.

"Ruthie, come on in. Didn't I tell you that it wasn't necessary for you to ever to knock? This is your home after all."

"I know you said that," Ruthie replied as she opened the door. "But I don't want you to feel as if you don't have your own private space in this home. As far as I am concerned, you should feel as if this is your home too. I was checking to see if you are all right because I heard you talking to yourself. I was afraid you were having a nervous breakdown or something like it, from the exhaustion and boredom of taking care of Mother," Ruthie added.

"Come here, Ruthie, and sit down on the bed, because I want to tell you something." Ruth patted the bed space next to her and gestured to Ruthie to come over and sit down.

Ruthie did as Ruth requested, very slowly lowering herself onto the side of Ruth's bed. Ruth grabbed Ruthie's hand and asked if she would soon be marrying Billy. It was hard for Ruthie to concentrate on what Ruth was saying because this was the first time she had really taken Ruth's hand for a long period of time. She was amazed at how soft her hand felt on top of her own calloused hand. Ruthie was also aware that she was feeling as if she had collided with one of the barbed wire fences surrounding her property, which always resulted in an electrical shock flooding her whole body.

Ruthie made herself concentrate on Ruth's words. "So, you see Ruthie, when you marry Billy, you won't need me around. And I want you to have a normal life with a good man who obviously adores you."

Ruthie didn't know what to say or how to respond. She was overcome with emotion as tears rolled down her checks. "Marry Billy! What makes you think I am marrying Billy?" Ruthie shouted.

"Didn't he ask you to marry him at the fish fry tonight? He told me he was going to ask you to marry him at the dance and not to worry about having a place to live after you were married because his mother really wanted me to work for her if I didn't get another teaching position," Ruth said while wiping away some tears.

"He said that, did he? And, his mother is the conspirator joining with Billy to get you out of my life. Don't you ever listen to Billy again about this. I think I put an end to his romantic ideas tonight. He did ask me to consider marriage, and all I could think about was how miserable I would make him in the years ahead. I am in love with someone else, so I could never give my heart to him."

Ruth looked concerned as she waited for Ruthie's next words. Who was this other love Ruthie had just mentioned for the first time? Could it be her? Ruth had gotten herself in trouble before for expressing just how she felt about things. Her mother had often admonished her that most people didn't want complete honesty from anyone, especially when it came to sensitive subjects.

Ruthie cleared her throat and rubbed some tears from her eyes with the sleeve of her blouse. "Ruth, I am in love with you. I think I fell in love with you the first day you walked through the farmhouse door. I know God put this love in my heart for you, and I hope that doesn't shock you. I am not exactly sure what this means for one woman to love another woman as a man might love a woman. No one ever discusses such things. I am smart enough to know I'd never reveal my feelings for you to anyone because they would surely tell me I needed electric shock therapy or institutionalization. But even with all that uncertainty, I need to tell you that all I want to do is hold you in my arms. I've felt that way for a long time," Ruthie admitted.

Without a moment's hesitation, Ruth sat up in the bed and drew Ruthie into her arms. "Ruthie, I thought you might love me, but I wasn't sure. I daydreamed a thousand times about you telling me that you loved me. It is something I never thought you would say. I knew we were fast friends and that you liked my company, but I constantly repressed my true desires." Ruth pulled Ruthie onto the bed next to her as she continued to keep her arms firmly placed around Ruthie. She kissed Ruthie with all the tenderness she had held in her heart. Ruthie responded with her own kisses and felt as if she was right where she had always belonged.

"Oh, my dear, dear, Ruth," Ruthie said as she continued to kiss Ruth passionately. Ruthie could feel the soft curves of Ruth's body as she snuggled into her arms. Tears welled up in Ruthie, and Ruth momentarily pulled back enough to look Ruthie straight in the face inquiring, "What are all these tears about?"

"My darling, haven't you ever seen tears of joy? Well, this is what they look like. It's as if I have found the other half of myself, most certainly the best part of me. I have felt my whole life like something was wrong with me. Even when lots of people were around, I felt like something was missing. Now I know that something was you. My heart is finally home forever," Ruthie said.

"What is the exact day today, Ruth?" Ruthie asked.

"It is now Saturday, August 23, 1952," Ruth replied quizzically.

"Well," said Ruthie with great conviction. "This shall forever be our anniversary, my darling."

Ruth continued to kiss Ruthie as Ruthie pulled Ruth into her arms. "Let's stay like this all night," Ruthie suggested.

She had just laid Ruth's head on her shoulder when Ruthie heard scratching at the door. Ruthie chuckled. "I am not sure how Jenny is going to feel about sharing me with you, but she might as well get used to it."

Ruthie quickly jumped out of the bed and opened the bedroom door for Jenny, who bounded into the room happily. Ruthie pulled the throw rug right next to her side of the bed and said to Jenny, "Well, Jenny, I guess we both have found a new bed, and this one is yours, girl."

Jenny looked at Ruthie, trying to understand what was happening but obediently lay down on the rug, her eyes following Ruthie as she got in Ruth's bed and once again placed Ruth's head on her shoulder as she caressed Ruth's soft, curly hair.

Chapter 9

The warmth of the first rays of the morning sun streaming through the white lace curtain of Ruth's room awakened Ruthie, who looked at the alarm clock and noticed it was an hour past milking time. Ruthie watched with joy as Ruth's chest rose and fell with each breath; Ruth remained fast asleep. She suddenly remembered every detail of the soft kisses and gentle hugs of the night before. She quietly slipped out of bed, urging Jenny to follow along behind. Before she could stop Jenny, she watched as the dog jumped up where Ruthie had been sleeping and cuddled next to Ruth.

Ruthie moved quickly but quietly out the door with a big smile on her face. How *about that?* she thought. *That dog must love Ruth as much as I do. I always thought Jenny was a good judge of character.*

After Ruthie shut Ruth's door, Ruth awoke with the shock that it was an hour past the time she would check on Mrs. Stein. Ruth wasted no time in getting dressed and down to Mrs. Stein. She was pleased to see Mrs. Stein had not awakened yet, and so she proceeded into the kitchen to get the light breakfast fare for Mrs. Stein as she thought about the miracle of last night. Maybe God did answer prayers after all.

When she returned with the breakfast tray for Mrs. Stein, she realized she could not awaken her with her voice or gentle nudges. Ruth put her head right on Mrs. Stein's chest and could hear no heartbeat; nor could she detect any sign of breath. She went immediately to the phone. "Billy can you get Doc Ralph and bring him here immediately? I think Mrs. Stein has passed away. I took her breakfast tray into her room, and she is not breathing. I haven't even told Ruthie yet. She is out in the barn doing the morning chores."

"Oh my God, Ruth. I'll take care of everything, and as soon as I pick up the doc, I'll be right over. Are you afraid to tell Ruthie by yourself?" Billy inquired.

"No, Billie, I can do that. Lord knows I've been through this twice myself, and Ruthie has been through this once before. I can take care of her," Ruth assured Billy.

"Then go right to the barn and tell her I am on my way over with Doc Ralph and that my brother can finish any chores she has left," Billy insisted.

As Ruth walked slowly to the barn on this bright and humid late August morning, she knew the chemistry between the two of them would give way to this sad milestone she had to report to Ruthie. They had both chatted about Mrs. Stein sleeping more and her disinterest in eating for the past week. Ruthie had known the end was near for her mother. As Ruth walked into the barn with Jenny trailing along, she saw Ruthie carrying a bucket of milk to the milk house. Ruth quietly followed behind her without saying a word.

Ruthie thought she was daydreaming again about last night as she got a whiff of lavender in the air. She turned around to see Ruth sadly staring at her, tears running down her cheeks. Ruthie understood what Ruth was about to report, and said, "She's gone, isn't she, Ruth?"

Ruth walked over to Ruthie and clapped her arms around her, crying softly. Ruthie's thoughts returned to last evening. While she was finding the love of her life, her mother had decided to depart. It was almost providential. Curiously, she felt no guilt about having held Ruth last night as her mother drew her last breath. Her mother would not have to feel any more disappointment about her daughter who had never provided her with grandchildren and dressed too casually for Alma Stein's tastes. Yet it hit Ruthie that she was now an orphan and the only one left in her immediate family. Thank God, she was now Ruth's companion. This would take away, in large measure, the sting of the loss.

After Ruthie called the funeral home and her mother was removed from the home, she sat at the kitchen table in a daze. Ruth knew it would be a long day for all and made a pot full of coffee while putting out some huckleberry muffins for the taking. Once her cousin Billy and Aunt Bessie had left, she sat down next to Ruthie and held her hand. "I am so sorry, Ruthie. I know what it feels like to be an orphan. What can I do to help? Are their relatives you want me to call?" Ruth inquired.

Ruthie looked up at Ruth, and Ruth saw the tears. "If you could pick out a pretty dress for Mother, that would be a big help. You know better than I what would look best for Mother. I need to get it to the undertaker tomorrow. As for relatives, there is only one to call, whom I prefer never to call. But, there is no avoiding the task. That would be Father's sister, Aunt Mable, who lives down in Binghamton. As you know, all Mother's siblings are deceased, and her nieces and nephews, my cousins, live close by. I am sure your Aunt Bessie has already called every one of them already." Ruthie sighed.

"So why is calling Aunt Mable such a task?" Ruth asked.

Ruthie explained, "Aunt Mable married very well to a wealthy car dealer in Binghamton. She is quite nosy and manipulative. Mother could not abide her and often said the only reason her marriage lasted was because my Uncle Henry spent such long days at the dealership to avoid her. I'll have to invite her to stay with me, just as I did when Father died. I'm afraid you and I will have to play the game of staying in our separate bedrooms at night because there is no sneaking around Aunt Mable. She should have been a detective," Ruthie said.

"That's no problem, Ruthie. I completely understand. Of course, it must be that way. I'll do my best to charm your aunt and resume my habit of reading in bed to fall asleep. We'll survive, sweetheart," Ruth assured her love.

"Maybe you will survive but not me," Ruthie complained. "Aunt

Mable will be asking all kinds of questions about what I plan to do with the farm and what Mother and Father's last will provides about the disposition of the farm and hinting that she should get something since this was the farm she and my father shared as children."

With that, Ruthie got up and went to the phone to call Aunt Mable. Ruthie never procrastinated doing irksome tasks. She had learned long ago that, the longer you put off such duties, the more ominous they seemed to be.

When she got off the phone, she told Ruth that Aunt Mable would arrive in two days without Uncle Henry. "This is a very busy time of the year for the car business and he can't break away right now," Aunt Mable had remarked. Aunt Mable indicated she would return to Binghamton the day after the funeral. She would be with them for three nights.

All became a blur as Ruthie moved through the funeral proceedings. There were the usual calling hours at the funeral home the day and evening before the church service and then the funeral service, burial, and customary meal in Fellowship Hall put on by the Methodist women. It was a tribute to Alma Stein that so many people packed themselves in the Four Corners Methodist Church for the funeral on a very hot and humid late August day. The outside thermometer at the Stein home had read ninety degrees before Ruthie, Ruth, and Aunt Mable headed off to the church. All the way to the church, Aunt Mable kept chattering about this and that, especially telling her niece that, if she needed one, "my Henry could get you a nice new car at a very low cost." She also added that it was, nevertheless, "amazing how neat and clean you've kept this old car."

Ruthie felt very irritated about having to sit in the front pew with Aunt Mable and her six cousins, since none of them had ever shown any real liking for her. Her beloved companion was sitting two rows back with the rest of the Packer family. This was where their secret love was not so wonderful. Ordinarily when a spouse's parent had died, the grieving spouse held hands with his or her better half for support and comfort. Ruthie wanted to be sitting next to Ruth, holding her hand.

When they all arrived at the cemetery, Ruth did give Ruthie a big hug, and Billy followed suit. Ruth and Billy then moved back from the grave. No one present thought that this was anything but "very sweet"—that Ruthie's two best friends wanted to comfort her as best they could. Many in the community had often discussed how curious it was that Ruthie would not marry Billy. Marrying a friend from childhood was very common and a good foundation for a long marriage. Given Ruthie's average looks and tomboyish ways, Billy was probably the only offer of marriage she would ever get. Most of the community speculated Ruthie didn't want the possibility of Billy taking over her farm once they were married. Others suggested that Ruthie was not the biggest fan of Bessie Packer, and Ruthie did not want to spend her whole marriage having to please two partners to the marriage.

As the pastor finished the burial service, all Ruthie could think about was that she only had one more night with Aunt Mable. As people were leaving the cemetery, she heard Aunt Mable say to a group of women, "Ruthie hasn't discussed that with me, but I would assume Ruth would be heading back to Cooperstown looking for another teaching position now that Alma is gone." Ruthie felt anger welling up inside her, and her face turned red. How dare Aunt Mable gossip in this manner about Ruthie's future? It was absolutely none of her business.

The late luncheon at Fellowship Hall was another ordeal. Ruthie did not feel like even being civil to Aunt Mable and was afraid of all the questions she may have stirred up in Four Corners. At least there was some relief from the afternoon heat in Fellowship Hall, since it was in the basement of the church and three good-sized fans were circulating the air.

Ruth was busy helping the Methodist women serve the luncheon when Ruthie approached her in the kitchen and said, loudly enough for everyone to hear, "Ruth, do you happen to have that little tin of Bayer aspirin in your purse? My head is just *pounding*."

Ruth knew this was a clue that Ruthie needed to talk to her urgently; Ruthie knew, after all, that Ruth couldn't take aspirin, as it tore up her stomach.

Ruth replied equally as loudly while taking Ruthie's arm, "Well of course you have a bad headache, my dear, what with this scorching heat and all the emotional strain of losing your mother. Just follow me to my purse." With that, she gently took Ruthie's arm and led her farther back into the recesses of the kitchen. Ruth got a glass from the church cabinet, filled it with water, and pretended to hand her companion an aspirin. "Ruthie, what is it, sweetheart?" she whispered.

"It's Aunt Mable. I heard her gossiping at the cemetery about whether you would be staying with me now that Mother no longer needs a caretaker. I am not in any way prepared to make up some story about why you would stay on," Ruthie quietly replied. With that, Ruthie began to cry. Just the suggestion she might lose Ruth filled her with pain.

"Now, Ruthie," Ruth whispered back as she put her arms around Ruthie, "I am one step ahead of you on all this. Let me deal with Aunt Mable until she leaves. I told all the women in this kitchen a half an hour ago that, since I had not found a teaching position, I would tell you I could stay on for a couple months to help you deal with the disposition of your mother's worldly goods and ease you into living alone. All the women seemed to think that was a great idea and said how 'Christian' of me it was to do so. Little do they know that what they see as a Christian act of kindness is a source of joy to me. They need never know the real reason I will be staying on. As for where the story leads from there, you and I are bright enough to write that story. But for now, this is our explanation," Ruth advised as she retrieved a Kleenex from her purse and handed it to Ruthie.

Several people at the luncheon tables saw Ruthie crying in the kitchen and observed the interaction between the two women. Mrs.

Packer commented, "My niece Ruth has such a way of soothing Ruthie, and Ruthie seems to listen to her about things more than she listens to anyone else. It is a tribute to Ruth that Ruthie feels comfortable crying in front of her."

The irony of those words was lost on the audience at the table because these words were true beyond Mrs. Packer's wildest imagination. Mrs. Packer went on to relate what a good influence Ruth had been for Ruthie in her manner of dress and decorum, which might well lead to men being more attracted to Ruthie.

Before leaving the church that afternoon, Billy asked Ruth whether she thought Ruthie would get upset if he arranged with some of the farmers' sons to help him with the milking and evening chores at the Stein farm. Ruth advised that it would be great for Billy to arrange for the evening work since Ruthie had such a bad headache. Ruth told Billy she planned to send Ruthie to bed as soon as they got home, adding in a whisper, "Her Aunt Mable drives her crazy." Billy chuckled and said he had heard that before from Ruthie. "I understand she is quite a gossip and chatterbox," he said as he observed Aunt Mable deep in yet another conversation with some Methodist women.

When Ruth, Ruthie, and Aunt Mable arrived back at the farm, Ruth mentioned to Ruthie that the evening chores and milking were being taken care of by Billy and some boys from Future Farmers of America and that Ruthie should go upstairs and lie down for a couple hours. Aunt Mable was all in favor of that plan since she said she wanted "some more time to chat with Ruth." Surprisingly, Ruthie put up no resistance to the plan and headed slowly up the stairs to her drab bedroom with Jenny tailing behind. Ruthie knew Ruth could hold her own with Aunt Mable and probably come up with even more reasons for Ruth staying on at the Stein farm.

"I have some cold iced tea in the refrigerator if you would like some?" Ruth inquired. "We can even go out and sit on the front porch, where I noticed a cooling breeze was drifting in from the north."

"Don't mind if I do accept your hospitality," Aunt Mable said. "I like two teaspoons of sugar in my tea," she directed. Aunt Mable went ahead to the front porch and sought out the most comfortable chair among the wicker furniture and awaited Ruth.

Meantime, Ruth got out a small plate and put some of her sugar cookies from yesterday, which she had noticed Aunt Mable couldn't resist.

Once both women were seated, Aunt Mable began her interrogation. "How wonderful it has been for Ruthie to have your help these past six months as my sister-in-law was dying. I suppose you are quite anxious to get back to Cooperstown. There is so much more going on there than in this little hick town of Four Corners," Mable added just before taking a big swig of her iced tea.

Ruth smiled and said, "There are many good things to be said about Four Corners, and I haven't really minded being here. You must know your niece is a special lady, with high standing in this community. She is very intelligent, making conversation very easily about things that most people in Four Corners don't even know about. I will miss Ruthie when I leave, and I hope she will stay in contact with me. Perhaps she can even visit me in Cooperstown sometime," Ruth added

Ruth went on to explain that she wouldn't be leaving for a couple of months as she saw to the disposition of Alma's worldly goods and Ruthie finished harvesting the crops. This would take some of the sting out of Mrs. Stein's death for Ruthie as she adjusted to life without her mother.

Aunt Mable said she could well understand how busy Ruthie would be with the corn silage, wheat, and resulting straw yet to be bailed and mowed. "Say, Ruth, while you are going through Alma's personal effects, would you look to see if you can find a beautiful butterfly pin my mother gave Alma when she married my brother? It looks like a monarch butterfly, and Ruthie does not seem like the type of woman who would give a hoot about jewelry," Aunt Mable observed.

Ruth had seen the nosy side of Aunt Mable. Now she was observing the manipulative and greedy side. Ruthie loved her mother's butterfly pin and had told Ruth that she would like Ruth to have it "because it will look just so beautiful on you, and we can remember how close you were to my mother before she died."

Ruth decided to tackle this request head-on. "Truth be told, Ruthie gave me that pin the morning Alma died. She said she wanted me to have it because she realized how close Alma and I had become in her last days. I can ask Ruthie if she wants me to hand it over to you, if you wish?" While Ruth knew Aunt Mable was greedy, she instinctively knew Aunt Mable was also the type of woman who would not want to be perceived as greedy. Oh no. Ruth! Don't bother asking Ruthie about that silly old pin. You certainly earned the right to wear it given all the care you gave Alma. Ruthie was quite right to give it to you," Aunt Mable replied.

Chapter 10

Aunt Mable was on her way to Binghamton by midmorning, after she had consumed one last enormous breakfast and had taken several sticky buns for the eating on her car trip.

At the breakfast table that morning, Ruthie had her turn at matching wits with Aunt Mable. Aunt Mable had said, "Isn't Jenny *your* dog, Ruthie? Every morning when I get up to use the bathroom, that dog has been parked outside Ruth's bedroom and not yours. Why is that?"

Without skipping a beat, Ruthie replied, "It's the truth that Jenny has been spoiled to death by Ruth and now awaits her new friend's breakfast scraps. Going to the barn with me is no longer on Jenny's agenda. You can see how much people seem to gravitate to Ruth; it's even more so with cats and dogs. The feral cats who drink milk at the barn even let Ruth pick them up when they would scratch me to death. She just has a way with all God's creatures."

With that explanation, Aunt Mable got up and headed to her car.

"Make sure you say hi to Uncle Henry for me," Ruthie shouted as Aunt Mable pulled out of the driveway.

When Ruthie was convinced Aunt Mable was clearly out of sight, she went back into the house to find Ruth, who was starting some laundry in the garage. Ruthie put her arms around the back of Ruth as Ruth was placing the clothing in the washing machine. "Thank God that nightmare has passed!" she exclaimed.

"Now we need to get back to sweet dreams," Ruth replied.

The two women hugged each other. Ruth gave Ruthie a very long and satisfying kiss.

Ruthie went out to the barn to finish the morning chores. When she came in at noontime, she saw a note on the table from Ruth. "Off to pick some blackberries. I want to make you a blackberry pie for supper. Your sandwich is in the refrigerator, along with some lemonade."

Ruthie was glad Ruth had escaped the house for a few hours after the prison it had become with Aunt Mable visiting. How like Ruth to turn her thoughts to Ruthie's favorite dessert. Ruth would probably pick many quarts of blackberries and sell some to the neighbors who didn't have blackberry bushes. She did this to earn a little extra spending money, although Ruthie wished she didn't have to do it because it sometimes caused Ruth's arms to get scratched from the thorns on the bushes. Ruthie ate her sandwich, grabbed a date-filled cookie, and took a brief nap before the afternoon chore of bringing the cows up from the pasture and placing them in their stalls for milking.

As Ruth prepared supper that night, she realized how much she longed to be in bed with Ruthie. She wondered if it was too soon for Ruthie to even consider such intimacy. She had pondered over the last few days whether it was a bad omen for their physical relationship to have begun on the very night Mrs. Stein was dying in the room below. Ruthie had been giving her a hug or quick kiss when others, particularly Aunt Mable, were not around, but Ruthie seemed quite preoccupied about something else.

After this night's supper, Ruth decided it was worth the risk to ask Ruthie how she felt about this coincidence. "Sweetheart, how are you doing? You seem quieter than usual?"

"Ruth, don't worry about me. I will be fine. I knew Mother's death was imminent. If I seem quieter than usual, it's because I realize my whole birth family has passed away, and I'm the one left with all the memories. Thank God you have been right here, standing beside me, holding me the night after Mother died, because I would feel impossibly alone without you," Ruthie explained as tears rolled down her cheeks.

"It doesn't bother you that our first night together in bed was the very night your mother died?" Ruth asked.

"Honey," Ruthie replied as she put down her coffee cup and took Ruth's hand, "what has occurred to me is that my old life passed away that night Mother went home to God, so I could start my new life with you unencumbered. It is as if God perfectly put you in my life at the exact time when I needed you the most, and I no longer feel the need to please Mother."

Ruth got up from her chair, walked toward Ruthie, held out her hand to Ruthie, and said, "The dishes can wait tonight."

They headed up the stairs to Ruth's bedroom, slowly undressed, and crawled under the bedsheets. They instantly moved into each other's arms and began kissing one another with more passion than the first night they had experimented.

As Ruth's soft hands moved to Ruthie's breasts, Ruthie felt an indescribable wave of intense pleasure throughout her body. She encouraged Ruth not to stop her exploration and could feel a tingling between her legs she had never experienced. Ruthie instinctively guided Ruth's fingers between her thighs. Ruthie felt a wave of passion she had never felt before, followed by a feeling of complete release from every bit of tension in her body. Tears of joy once again rolled down Ruthie's cheeks.

Ruth sensed the pleasure Ruthie felt and gently kissed her lips and neck as she whispered, "Do you have any doubts about how attractive you are to me and how much love I have for you?"

Without saying a word, Ruthie rolled off her back, faced Ruth, and very cautiously returned all these same touches in the same places on Ruth's body, finally knowing what it meant to fully love a woman. She heard Ruth quietly repeating, "Yes, yes, yes," until Ruth's body tensed a bit and then exploded into pleasure.

After cradling one another for several minutes, enjoying the softness of their bodies together, Ruth smiled at Ruthie and said, "I had a feeling this might be wonderful, but only because it was you who was loving me. I never had sex with a man because there was no emotional connection when we kissed or petted a bit. You were the one I was waiting for—physically strong yet tender, unafraid to let yourself be completely vulnerable to me. How could this love for one another be wrong?" she added.

"I have been giving our physical relationship a lot of thought since we first held each other the night Mother died and again the next night before Aunt Mable arrived. I know most of the world sees physical love between two women as unnatural and wrong. You don't even hear anyone ever talking about it as a possibility. However, I firmly believe God created this love just for us. I thought about growing up on this farm and observing all the life about me and concluded there are beautiful exceptions in nature to what is often considered normal."

Ruthie continued, "When I was very young and was told about four-leaf clovers, I would sometimes spend hours looking over patches of clover for just one. Usually, if I was persistent enough, I would find one among the hundreds of three-leaf clovers. They were so rare, yet they brought such hope and beauty. There they were, sprinkled sparingly about that large field, four leaves, perfectly balanced. For many, such as the Irish, they represent good fortune. God surely intended to make a few four-leaf clovers, just as He made three leaf clovers. We may be rare, Ruth, but we are not unnatural," Ruthie concluded.

"What a beautiful thought, sweetheart. Too bad we cannot share your reflections with the whole world."

With that comment, Ruth gave Ruthie one last lingering kiss and then turned on her left side to drift off to sleep. Ruthie, in turn, moved onto her left side, slipping her arms around Ruth with the knowledge that this would be the way they would sleep for the rest of their lives. Both women drifted off to sleep.

When Ruthie came in from the barn the next morning, it was well past the usual breakfast hour. She had floated through the chores with little effort, recalling how wonderful it had been to hold and be held by Ruth. She thought God had given her an immense blessing. She thought about how her rural community could never even imagine how two women could make each other so happy. She had no doubt whatsoever that God had brought Ruth to her, and she would move heaven and earth to keep them together.

As she entered the kitchen, she smelled coffee and cinnamon in the air, noting Ruth had made her delicious cinnamon buns. Ruth was frying some eggs and bacon, and when she saw Ruthie, she put down her utensils, pulled the pans off the burners, and walked over to Ruthie, taking Ruthie's hands as she stared into Ruthie's eyes. "Was I too forward last night, Ruthie?" she implored.

Ruthie leaned down and kissed Ruth and then gathered her in her arms for a gentle hug. "My dear, if that was too forward, you may continue to be so for the rest of our lives," Ruthie said. "You made a very special breakfast this morning. You must think I need more encouragement to fall in love with you. I think it just may be that we stole each other's hearts forever last night!" she concluded with a broad smile.

Ruthie sat at the table as Ruth poured her some coffee and finished cooking their breakfast. Ruthie was very curious about Ruth's natural and relaxed actions in bed last night. "Ruth, who taught you to kiss like that? I feel like you have kissed a woman before," Ruthie observed.

Ruth put down her fork and looked intently at Ruthie. "Well, Ruthie, English wasn't all I learned at Smith. There was this girl who pursued me my senior year when others were not around to see us together. She was a very precocious junior with auburn hair and almost as tall as you. Although we often held hands out of sight of others as we took long walks in the woods, nothing more happened between us until one day while we were hiking. She spun me around by a tree and started to kiss me. I had kissed some boys in my high school and college days, but I knew this was different and more pleasing. I kissed back, and then we just stopped. We never spoke about the incident again, and while I was attracted to her, I knew there was no future for us, so I just avoided her until I graduated. Does this bother you, Ruthie?"

Ruthie wanted to measure her words carefully in reply. "Well, it makes me a little jealous. But I guess we all have stolen a kiss here and there if we are half-alive. I kissed your cousin Billy a couple times out back of our respective barns when I was seven or eight. He seemed shocked at the time, but when we hit junior high, he asked me if he could kiss me one night after a church ice cream social. It was nice but nothing spectacular. Billy and I will always be best of friends. I do love him like a brother and often wondered as a child why God had put Walter Junior in our family instead of Billy," Ruthie said.

"Well he does think the world of you; that's for sure, "Ruth observed. "Throughout high school when we had family reunions, he'd talk about how smart you were and even said it was too bad you weren't going off to Smith like I was going to do. He talked about how strong you were and that he'd seen you outwork many men in haying season and how amazing it was that you seemed to enjoy farm work. I began to think you must be an Amazon woman." Ruth laughed.

"I hate to be ignorant, Ruth, but what is an Amazon woman?" Ruthie inquired, adding, "That doesn't sound like a compliment."

Ruth laughed and explained. "You are not ignorant because you don't know about Amazon women. Our civilization is not about to promote Amazon women. At Smith, I learned that they were Greek mythical women warriors, although there is some evidence that some women warriors existed at the height of the Greek and Roman empires. They were ferocious in battle. It was believed these women formed colonies where men were not allowed to live. To preserve their kind, once a year, they would visit a neighboring male colony to conceive. If the child any of the women bore was female, they kept her. But once a male child was beyond infancy, he was adopted by the neighboring paternal tribe," Ruth advised.

"No wonder I never heard about them from high school history, and certainly not in Sunday School!" Ruthie said.

With that, they both started laughing hilariously.

"I've discovered you are not an Amazon, Ruthie. You are a big teddy bear, not a fierce killing machine." And with that comment she got up from her seat and gave Ruthie a peck on the cheek before picking up their breakfast dishes to wash.

"So back to this kissing experience at Smith," Ruthie continued. "Were you in love with this gal?"

Ruth put down the plate she was washing, grabbed the coffee pot, and refilled both their cups. She sat down across the breakfast table and smiled at Ruthie. "You are the person God intended for me, Ruthie. Last night, while you held me in your arms, it was all the proof I needed to convince me that you are the one love I was meant to have by God's very plan. You are the only woman I have ever touched like I did last night, and as far as I am concerned, we were both what you could call virgins last night. We have been together in this house for six months, and we just naturally floated through each day without a harsh word between us, going about our daily chores effortlessly. We have broken bread together three times a day at this table, laughing and talking to one another as if we had known each other forever. It would never have been that easy with the girl at Smith. She was sort of arrogant and from a very wealthy family, which had high expectations of her marrying well. Her kiss that one time was experimental. There was nothing tentative about your kisses last night, and I knew how much you loved me from those tears of joy, as you called them," Ruth concluded with her charming smile.

Ruthie grabbed Ruth's hand from across the table, brought it to her lips for a kiss, and smiled. "Well, I had better call your cousin and see about bailing up my second cutting of alfalfa today. I am a whole week behind in putting away this second cutting because of Mother's death. Those gals in the pasture sure do like alfalfa when they are cooped up in the barn for the winter. I cut it all down for drying and raking two days ago. The weatherman says it will rain for sure late tomorrow, so the time to get it bailed is now," Ruthie added with a sense of urgency in her voice.

Ruth commented, "I suppose I am to blame for your late start this morning. I think maybe we should go to bed a little bit earlier each night now, don't you think, my dear?" With that, she winked at Ruthie and proceeded to the sink to finish her chores.

Ruth realized she should do some extra baking in case they were likely to have extra farmhands to feed for dinner. It was wonderful how all the small farmers helped each other get their crops in each year. One farmer might have a mower, as well as a baler, yet another farmer might have a combine. They often shared farm equipment, and when it was time to harvest the hay, they all helped each other. The farmers with teenage sons made sure they shared this physical wealth with the farmers who didn't. But it had become a tradition for each farm wife to cook big meals at noon and at five to sustain all that muscle power.

She didn't mind at all being Ruthie's "wife" and doing her part to please the male guests with meat, potatoes, and snap beans from the garden, topped off with pie and lemonade. This task she had already performed in late June during the first cutting and baling of hay. The five men around her table were ecstatic about her cooking and always thanked her profusely. Ruthie later told her that, after the baling was done and the last meal consumed, Mr. Packer had told her, "Ruthie, that niece of mine has to be the best cook in our family, but don't tell my wife I said that! Promise?" "Mum's the word, Mr. Packer," Ruthie had told him. "You can see I've gained a little weight since Ruth's been cooking for me."

"Well, don't worry about putting on a little weight, Ruthie. I always liked pleasingly plump women, and with the physical work you do, a few extra pounds ain't going to hurt you one bit," he'd assured Ruthie, adding. "I know your father is looking down from heaven right now beaming with pride at how you've been able to keep up this farm."

Ruth stopped her daydreaming and finished her chores at the sink. The kitchen sink faced the entrance of the barn, and every time Ruthie could be seen walking to the barn, Ruth marveled at Ruthie's stature and confident walk to the place where Ruthie was most at home. Ruthie may be ill at ease with some people at church functions, but she was self-confident about her farming skills and her animals. Ruth had helped her in the barn occasionally when Ruthie was down with a cold or had a flulike illness. This was always over Ruthie's objection, but Ruth always replied, "You want to deny me the right to spend more time with you?"

On another occasion, Ruth had reasoned with Ruthie that the heavier physical work kept Ruth in shape to lift the heavy iron skillet that made most of their hot food. It had also given her the muscle to more easily move Mrs. Stein up and down from her bed. To this reasoning Ruthie had replied, "Maybe I like you just the way you are with no changes. It would be a crying shame for you to become a muscular miniature of me and lose those wonderfully soft hands of yours."

And so, the banter would often go back and forth between the two women. Both were witty and kind in their remarks to one another, and it was another sign they were meant for one another. Sharp words were rarely exchanged between the two, unless either of them thought the other was taking on too much work or church duties to fit the wishes of the other.

Around ten o'clock that morning, Billy pulled into the Stein driveway with the Packer baler and his brother John in tow. Ruth went out the screen door and waived at Billy, shouting that Ruthie was out back by the hayloft checking out the conveyer.

"Will you be ready, cousin, with a hungry crew of six about 12:30?" Billy needled Ruth.

"When have I ever left you less than three pounds heavier after one of my meals? You just go whip up an appetite helping my land-lord," Ruth shouted back.

Ruth got busy with all she had to do. Peeling endless potatoes, husking some sweet corn, pulling the pork chops out of the icebox for frying after coating them with her special bread crumb coating, while all the time watching the oven to pull out the two loaves of bread and apple cobbler was quite a task. Sometimes she even thought she could open a diner and have less work. She had gotten up during the June farmhand days in the morning at the same time as Ruthie to do all this preparation for the farmhands' noon feast, while also preparing the breakfast for the two of them and Mrs. Stein.

The routine was set for the rest of the crop season. Ruthie helped her neighbors get their hay, wheat, and corn silage harvested. In return, the neighbors helped her get all her crops stored away for the winter. Every noon that the neighbors arrived to help Ruthie, Ruth made sure they had a delicious meal to eat at noontime.

Each morning after breakfast, the two women would pull out the *Upper Room*, the Methodist devotional guide, continuing the Stein tradition of family devotions. Both women looked forward to this quiet time together before they hurried off to their respective duties, and it reminded them that, but for God's grace, they would never have met.

On one occasion when they were having devotions, they saw Billy at their front porch screen door and asked him if he would like to join them while they finished their devotions. He gladly accepted as Ruth poured him a cup of coffee and offered him a biscuit with butter and honey. This occasion became a blessing for the two women because Billy reported the incident to his mother, and she in turn told anyone in the church who would listen. No one in Four Corners would ever accuse Ruth and Ruthie of being hypocrites about their faith. They were discovered quietly praying to the Lord apart from the "public square" of the Sunday church service. This was something that could not be said of most members of their church.

Chapter 11

October 1952

It was just about two months after Alma Stein had passed, and Ruth was completing her last duties of cleaning the house from attic to basement of the unneeded personal possessions of Ruthie's parents. Many items were donated to the church for the annual garage sale. Ruth knew antiques, and so she sorted out the valuable items Ruthie should retain. At the church rummage sale, Mrs. Ella Jenkins, a relatively well-off woman of the church, approached Ruth and asked if Ruth might take a break with her and have a cup of coffee in Fellowship Hall. Ruth replied, "Sure." She informed her sister Methodist Fellowship members that she was taking a coffee break.

Once the two women were settled in their chairs with a cup of coffee and an oatmeal cookie, Mrs. Jenkins began, "You probably don't know that I am on our local public library board. Just last night, our current librarian, Florence Lincoln, told us she had to step down as librarian due to her age and concerns about getting around this winter. We will be advertising this position in *The Times*. However, I immediately thought of you. I know it is probably getting near the time you were going to move back to Cooperstown, and I do not want to meddle in your affairs. Because it is midyear and it is unlikely a teaching position may now be available for you in Cooperstown, I thought you might like this humble job to tide you over." Mrs. Jenkins smiled broadly at a woman whose intellect she clearly admired.

"My goodness, Ella, what an interesting offer. What are the hours involved and what would you expect of me?" Ruth asked.

"Well, the pay is modest to say the least, at only sixty dollars a week. The library is open Tuesdays through Fridays from 10:00 a.m. to 5:00 p.m. and on Saturdays from 10 a.m. to 3:00 p.m. It is closed on Sundays of course, as well as all school holidays. You are the staff, so you would be checking out the books, readying books for distribution, collecting overdue fines, and restocking bookshelves. I thought you might have a children's reading hour on Saturdays. Mrs. Lincoln didn't quite have the personality to do that, but I know you would," Mrs. Jenkins explained.

Ruth sat quietly for a moment and had two thoughts. First, this would be a great way for her to stay with Ruthie without explanation, and it would also mean an extra $240 a month income for the two of them. "I am very much interested, and you may tell the library board about my interest. Let me know what they decide," Ruth said.

When Ruth got home from the rummage sale, she started cooking Ruthie's favorite supper, which included fried chicken, mashed potatoes, and canned string beans from their garden. Ruth whipped up some biscuits too and got out the butter, so it would melt perfectly on the biscuits. How Ruthie loved butter. No margarine was used in the Stein household. All the local farmers saw margarine as a direct threat to their milk production.

Ruth wanted everything to be perfect when she told Ruthie about the possible library position. She knew Ruthie was prideful about supplying the couple's financial needs and sometimes jealous when Ruth chose to be away from the farm without her.

As Ruthie walked into the kitchen at 5:30 p.m., she was elated with the smell of fried chicken and fresh biscuits. The table had been set with the Sunday china. "For goodness sakes, Ruth, what's the special occasion?" Ruthie asked.

"Your presence in this kitchen is always a special occasion, my love. Just sit down and relax," Ruth suggested.

"I'm beginning to think your last name is O'Connor and not Packer when you give me blarney like that. Something's up. I just know it. Don't tell me we've been invited to go somewhere I'd prefer not to go, or Aunt Mable is coming back for another visit," Ruthie moaned.

"No, my dear. It is something uplifting. Give me a minute to put the food on the table, and I'll tell you what it is," Ruth said. With great dispatch, Ruth placed the delicious fare on the table. She took Ruthie's hand as they said their usual blessing and then passed the chicken to Ruthie.

"Well, you've gotten me very curious, sweetheart. What is so exciting that it deserves a meal on the Sunday china?" Ruthie asked as she put a large pad of butter on her mashed potatoes and biscuit.

Ruth never hemmed and hawed around Ruthie. She had learned in these past few months that Ruthie liked to get to the point of every serious conversation quickly. "At the church rummage sale today, Ella Jenkins took me aside and asked me if I would consider becoming the Four Corners public librarian. It is not sure that I would be selected. She needs the library board's approval, but I have a feeling Mrs. Jenkins holds sway over the board," Ruth said.

"She certainly does have a lot of power on that board and many other boards, given all her money. I will say, though, that we wouldn't even have a library but for her generosity. Probably our church doors might not be open either but for her yearly tithe," Ruthie observed.

"Yes, money is power. That has always been the case and will always be the case. But I would say Mrs. Jenkins isn't an arrogant person. She doesn't appear to throw her weight around at church and seems quite friendly with the pastor, who is not one to mince words," Ruth said.

The wheels in Ruthie's mind were whirling so fast she didn't know what to say. She would miss Ruth's presence on the farm during the days the library was open. She would not take any money from Ruth for household expenses. However, she knew above all else she wanted

Ruth to be happy, and Ruth was the happiest when she got a chance to be with the public, chatting up a storm with all kinds of people. Ruthie also knew Ruth would be a natural as a librarian. Who could ever surpass a Smith College English major for knowledge of the literary world?

It seemed like an eternity for Ruth as she awaited Ruthie's comments. "Is this something you really want to do, my dear? Or are you just trying to find any way you can to help with our finances? How much does this job pay?"

"I would be getting $60 a week which would be an additional $240 a month for us. But that is not the reason I would take the position. This would be a chance to keep up my knowledge of current literature and maybe even help some students who would stop by to improve their grades by pointing them to the right books for their term papers," Ruth said.

"That is all certainly true. The board should be paying you more. Will the library have its usual hours of operation?" Ruthie asked.

"Yes. Nothing would change around here, except I would leave your lunch in the refrigerator. Since I don't have to be there until 10:00 a.m., I can make sure we have a good breakfast together and do all the household chores that need to be done before I leave. Dinner will be planned ahead of time, and we can eat at 6:30 p.m. instead of 6 p.m. if that is okay?" Ruth said.

"My dear, I don't own you. All I want for you is to be happy, and I can see the possibility of this position really excites you. I have often thought that, given your gregarious personality, it must get pretty lonely for you in this old farmhouse," Ruthie said as she rolled her eyes about the ancient kitchen.

"I have no complaints, Ruthie. You know I often wander out to the barn to talk with you and help where I can. Sometimes when I come out to the barn, I feel like I am intruding on your private world and slowing you down from your chores," Ruth said.

Ruthie laughed, thinking about their recent afternoon in the haymow. "Haven't I always been elated to see your beautiful face appear in my 'private world,' as you call it, each time you've come to the barn? In fact, I seem to recall a time quite recently when I showed you how the haymow could be used for things other than storing hay," Ruthie said, smiling broadly.

Ruth joined Ruthie in her laugh and said, "You surely did. It is a memory I will hold forever."

Ruthie looked directly into Ruth's eyes and said, "There is every reason you should take this job, but I want you to know your pay needs to go into your separate bank account. I will not take one penny of it. You already contribute to our financial situation by your wise store purchases, your labor in doing all our housework, gardening, and taking care of the chickens, as well as canning all these vegetables and fruits for use in the winter. I will never be able to repay you for all your work around here. It has always made me feel like a full partner to you by working the farm and selling the milk to the cooperative. I know we don't have very much extra money for the niceties of life, and I am sorry about that. Maybe now you can buy yourself something occasionally."

The conversation was gong better than Ruth had anticipated. She had guessed correctly that Ruthie wanted to be the provider. She would handle the pay issue carefully. "Oh, sweetheart, you have been most generous with me when it comes to money. Every time I head out this door to go shopping, you ask me if I need more money. The library pay will just help me feel better about myself. After all, what was four years at Smith all about unless the good Lord wanted me to use my brain to enlighten a few human beings about the important aspects of life? I've talked your ears off these last few months about this and that. I have been blessed to have such an intelligent companion who seems happy to hear my ramblings on the state of the world," Ruth said.

"You never ramble on about anything, Ruth. Every word that comes out of that cute little mouth of yours has meaning and purpose.

Sometimes I feel like I'm getting a college education just listening to you," Ruthie replied with conviction.

"So, I guess I am to tell Ella Jenkins I'd be glad to become the Four Corners librarian. I'll phone her tomorrow morning," Ruth said.

After dinner was over and the dishes cleared, Ruthie said, "Come here, sweetheart." She opened her arms for one of the hugs she reserved just for Ruth. Ruth was happy to oblige. And as Ruth gave her a big kiss, Ruthie once again felt that special chemistry between them.

Chapter 12

June 1953

The invitation arrived one month before the June wedding. After a ten-month courtship, Billy was finally marrying the beautiful and sweet Cindy Adams whom Ruthie had suggested he pursue. Both Ruth and Ruthie were very happy for Billy because Cindy was a "catch" and they suspected Cindy had been infatuated with Billy for some time. They knew Billy's mother must be ecstatic because she was desperate to have grandchildren, and a third-generation heir to the Packer farm.

"Are we going?" Ruthie inquired as she finished her supper and placed her dishes in the sink.

"Well of course we are going!" Ruth exclaimed. "This is my first cousin and your lifelong friend," Ruth curtly replied. "Why wouldn't we go?"

Ruthie was a bit taken aback by Ruth's tone. "It's just that I have always disliked attending weddings. First, I hate having to get all dressed up, and second, it is a purely heterosexual event that reminds me I am an old maid in the eyes of the community, a woman to be pitied and placed at a table in the back of the reception room," Ruthie complained.

"My goodness, we are grouchy today, aren't we?" Ruth responded. "Look, Ruthie, your Sunday best will be fine for this occasion, and this is not a wedding where we will be seated in a back-row table. I am a first cousin, and you are Billy's best friend, so there is no way we will be seated at some remote table. I am very friendly with Cindy, and she will see to it that we are near the front if that is what you want," Ruth promised.

"Well, I am sure you will enjoy talking to Cindy. Don't think I haven't watched the interactions between you two. If I didn't know better, I would think you are sweet on her, and she on you," Ruthie snapped.

"Now I must say that's the first time I've seen the green monster emerge from you," Ruth declared. "Where did that remark come from? Of course, I enjoy being friends with Cindy. She is one of the few people in our community who stops by our humble little library every week for new books, and she is extremely well read. I enjoy conversing with her always. And is it so wrong to be friends with a blond?" Ruth asked with a grin.

"Sorry, Ruth. I was wrong to have said that," Ruthie quickly replied. "If I am honest with you, I must tell you I feel so inadequate to be around you in public places. You are always dressed to the nines, and I am just an old plain-Jane compared to you. People are always asking me why you haven't gotten married, and sometimes I even convince myself that would have been a better life for you," Ruthie explained with downcast eyes.

"Sweetheart, you must stop considering what others in this community may think about us. I have had several women in the church ask me why I wasn't married yet. I simply tell them that none of the men I have ever dated measured up to my father. This is somewhat true. If I had allowed myself to fall into society's expectations about who I should be sleeping with every night, it would have to have been someone like my father, who valued my mind and was a complete gentleman. Even then, marriage to such a man would have left me wanting for someone like you, someone who was as concerned about my sexual satisfaction as much as her own, and someone who emotionally fulfilled me. That person is you, Ruthie, and it always will be." Ruth got up from the table and headed toward the staircase.

"Now we will look in your closet to see what you must wear, and if we don't find something appropriate, there is still plenty of time for a quick trip to dress shops in Watertown. I think we can afford to buy you a new dress. Lord knows, I'd like to see a new dress on you." Ruth laughed.

"So, you don't like being seen with me in church with the three dresses I alternate each week?" Ruthie pouted.

"For goodness sake, we are a bit irritable today, aren't we," Ruth spit back. "You know it is not your clothes that matter to me, and I am proud to be around you in your overalls. But there is nothing wrong with getting all dressed up for a big occasion like Billy's wedding, and you never buy yourself anything new. I know our budget is tight, but it's not that tight. I've saved up quite a bit of money from selling eggs and blackberries, so this dress will be my gift to you for being my cousin's best friend all these years, which eventually culminated in our meeting," Ruth reasoned.

They did not find anything appropriate in Ruthie's closet, as Ruth knew they wouldn't. Within two days, they were off to Emerson's in Watertown, which was considered the place where all the well-heeled ladies shopped. The store was also known for being the only store in Watertown with an elevator. It was sort of ridiculous to have an elevator because there were only two floors in the store, but heaven forbid, the wealthy should have to climb upstairs to see their best dresses.

As they walked into the store, a woman greeted them with a big smile and the offer of assistance. "How may I be of help today, ladies? Is there anything you need? Or are we just window-shopping today?" the saleswoman asked.

"We are looking for a special dress for my friend here, who has been invited to her best friend's wedding. As you can see my friend is quite tall and sometimes has trouble finding a dress, but I just knew Emerson's could fit the bill," Ruth replied with authority.

"Well yes, I am sure we can. Come with me, I think I have just the ticket. How lovely that your friend is getting married, dear," the saleslady gushed. "How long have you been friends with the bride?" she inquired.

Before Ruth could speak up, Ruthie barked out, "It's not a she, it is a he who is my best friend."

"Oh, how interesting that you have a man in your life you call your best friend. Not many women can say that. A woman's best friend is usually a woman like this nice lady with you today. How unusual," the saleslady said.

"Well, what are you trying to say? That men and women cannot be best friends and nothing more?! That's a deplorable outlook and probably why women have not gotten as far in the world as they should because they are not allowed to make friends with men outside of marriage and garner their respect for having abilities beyond cooking and having children," Ruthie lectured.

Ruth was quite embarrassed by Ruthie's words and demeanor. It reminded her of some of the suffragettes who graduated from Smith before 1920. They were forever coming back to their alma mater year after year, lecturing about how deplorable life had been before women got the right to vote. It wasn't that she disagreed with them at all. It was just their strident tone didn't always seem to advance their cause in the 1930s. Ruth knew she had to step into this lecture before it got out of control. "They grew up together on neighboring farms and are the same age, so they went all through school together and just really hit it off," Ruth tried to explain.

"And you are not the one walking down the aisle with him? That must be a disappointment for him because you have such a stunning figure and beautiful eyes," the saleslady said as she tried to recover from her reprimand by Ruthie.

Ruthie didn't wait for Ruth to chime in again. Ruthie understood it was time for her to speak for herself. "I am a bit disappointed, but I didn't believe I was the one for Billy, and I told him so when he asked me to marry him some time ago. We were too much alike, which I think is not always the best marriage material. We are better off treating each other like a brother and sister," Ruthie explained.

Ruth knew Ruthie's answer made no sense at all to this woman, who was certainly prying into areas that should have been none of her concern. Ruth pressed on. "So, what do you have for this stunning woman, as you call her?"

"Well, I am imagining something in blue," the saleswoman suggested. She led them to a rack of dresses and pulled out one in a size 18. "Is this your size, dear?" she asked.

Ruthie indicated it was exactly her size and went off to the dressing room to try it on. Ruthie was certainly not one to spend time shopping for clothes. She tried on the blue dress, saw that it fit her figure quite well, and that was that.

When Ruthie emerged from the dressing room to look at herself in a full-length mirror, Ruth tried not to stare or seem more than just one friend complimenting another. But Ruthie's appearance had indeed stunned her as the saleswoman had predicted. "My goodness, Ruthie, you look grand, just simply grand," Ruth commented.

Had Ruthie gone to Smith and paraded around the campus in Pendleton's finest wool suits, she would have had to beat off all the other lesbians on campus to keep her as their girlfriend. It wasn't only true that "clothes made the man"; they often made the woman too.

"It has been a pleasure assisting you with this purchase," the saleswoman said as she carefully folded the dress into an Emerson's box. "Do you need any accessories to go with this beautiful dress?" she asked.

"I think she is all set with just the blue dress," Ruth answered quickly so Ruthie didn't say something more to the already befuddled clerk. "How much do we owe you?"

"Okay then, that will be $15.98," she replied.

Ruth had given Ruthie a twenty-dollar bill before they went into the store, assuring Ruthie that it would not be more than that, given

Emerson's recent advertisement in the *Watertown Daily Times*. Ruthie handed the clerk the twenty and said thank you when she received her change.

It did not take long for Ruthie to run to their car, Emerson's box in hand. Ruth could not keep up with Ruthie's long stride, so she didn't even try. Once in the passenger seat, she looked over at Ruthie and said, "I have never seen you so ill-tempered as you were with that salesclerk, Ruthie. It was embarrassing." Ruth then righted herself in the seat as she stared out the windshield.

"Look, Ruth. Do you think it was right for her to be interrogating me about the circumstances of my relationship with Billy? It was none of her business. She was dumbstruck over knowing that Billy and I were best friends. Isn't it all right for a woman and a man to be best friends?" Ruthie asked.

Ruth hesitated for a moment and then let out a big sigh. "She was just trying to make conversation while attempting to make a sale, Ruthie. You didn't need to be so curt with her. After all, she did make an accurate assessment that you are a stunning-looking woman. I'll make sure I never let you go into this store alone again, for fear she'll get you in her clutches." Ruth laughed.

"That is plain ridiculous, and you know it. She gave me a compliment to make a sale. You said so yourself," Ruthie countered.

"Maybe, maybe not," Ruth replied as she smiled at Ruthie. "I watched her try to figure you out as you walked in front of the large mirror. You looked quite dazzling to her I think, when you transformed yourself by taking off that old frock you have on today and stepping into the beautiful, blue dress. I didn't mind her comments about you being stunning, because you are, whether you choose to believe it or not, my dear," Ruth said.

Ruthie lightened up and then began laughing. "I guess I wasn't very friendly to her. I really don't know what got into me. I think it's that I am so tired of society's presumptions about who should be friends and who should be spouses. I couldn't tell her I had a new best friend, and that person was you. I couldn't tell her that it is possible to be both a best friend and a lover to one person. They are not mutually exclusive, you know?" Ruthie explained.

"Yes, sweetheart, you have taught me that is true, and I am glad to hear that I am still your best friend after dragging you into this hell they call Emerson's!" Ruth replied as she grabbed Ruthie's right hand and held it tightly.

———

The wedding was truly beautiful, both Ruth and Ruthie agreed. Cindy was radiant in her white wedding gown, and Billy smiled broadly as he watched his beloved come down the aisle. The small church was packed, with extra chairs placed in the back of the church as well as up and down the side aisles. There was not a cloud in the sky that day, and with the windows of the church open, a cooling breeze made the guests very comfortable.

Ruth observed that, next to Cindy, it was Ruthie who was getting all the stares and compliments. It was as if they'd all suddenly found a lovely lady who had been dwelling in their midst and had been overlooked for more than three decades. Ruthie was very self-conscious every time one of the wedding guests came up to her during the reception and gave her a compliment on how well she looked in the new blue dress. After the fifth or sixth compliment, Ruth whispered in her ear, "Stop looking so dumbfounded. Just say thank you and smile when they pay you a compliment. I know all this attention makes you uncomfortable, but you deserve it."

Just before the wedding cake was cut, Billy approached Ruthie and held out his arms. "I am honored you got all dressed up for this occasion, Ruthie. You look beautiful," he gushed.

Ruth saw Cindy smiling at the head reception table as Billy was expressing his thoughts to Ruthie. She saw no jealousy in Cindy's eyes. Since she and Cindy had become good friends after arriving in Four

Corners, Cindy knew from what Ruth had told her that Ruthie loved Billy like a brother and not a potential husband.

Ruth also sensed Cindy had let her mind consider the possibility that Ruth and Ruthie might be more than friends, although Ruth did nothing to encourage these thoughts. However, on one occasion, Cindy had said to Ruth, "I am so happy the two of you found one another. That's not easy to do in this little town." And yet another time, Cindy had expressed to Ruth that she should "hurry home to Ruthie, or she certainly will be worried about you." She was pleased her cousin was marrying a woman with such an open and warm heart.

Chapter 13

July 1953

Ruth and Ruthie were in the church parking lot when Mr. Salter, the new high school principal, asked if he might speak to Ruth after church. "Well, of course you may," Ruth said. As she accompanied Ruth into the sanctuary, Ruthie whispered, "What could that be about?" They sat down in their usual pew. "He is a bachelor you know. Maybe he wants to ask you out on a date?" she conjectured with a wink. Ruth rolled her eyes at Ruthie and proceeded to pick up the hymnal to look up the first hymn.

Once the service concluded, Ruth conferred with Mr. Salter in a corner of the narthex. "Ruth, with the recent consolidation of Four Corners School District with our neighboring two school districts, it seems we will be opening an additional teaching position in the English Department. I know from meeting you here at church that you are a Smith graduate and that you did teach English in Cooperstown. Would you be interested in teaching junior and senior English classes in September?" Mr. Salter asked.

Ruth was overwhelmed with joy. Now she had a legitimate reason to stay with Ruthie, and in addition, she'd be able to put her brain back to work full-time. She had loved every aspect of her teaching experience in Cooperstown. She had felt lost when she'd stepped aside for the Korean War veteran. Being with Ruthie had greatly softened the loss of that job. Nevertheless, the chance to introduce young minds to the best of English literature, as well as help them develop advanced writing skills, would give an additional purpose to her life. It would also be a way to help with household finances. The library job had been great and aided the household income somewhat. But now, she would probably spend fewer hours on the job, making good money. She wanted to take Ruthie on a vacation to New England and show her Smith College and the rocky Maine coast. She would be able to afford this luxury with summers off and more income.

"Yes, Mr. Salter, I am very interested," Ruth said.

"Well then, great. It is not often, if ever, a high school principal in this part of the woods gets to hire a Smith graduate. Can you come by my office tomorrow about 10:00 a.m. and bring your transcript from Smith, as well as your New York Regents certification?" Mr. Salter asked.

"I most certainly can," replied Ruth. With that, she extended her hand to Mr. Salter. She left the narthex and headed to the car, where Ruthie had all the windows down and was patiently waiting.

"So, when is your first date?" Ruthie inquired with a twinkle in her eye.

"Stop saying things like that," Ruthie scolded. "Wasn't I just singing 'It Had to Be You' last night while we were getting ready for bed? Mr. Salter had a better idea than dating me. He would like me to start teaching English classes in the fall," Ruth said with a direct glance at Ruthie.

Ruthie wanted to be happy for Ruth. She knew how brilliant her love was and how underutilized her mind had been these past months. She also instantly felt the possible loss of Ruth during the noontime hours. "My goodness, Ruth," Ruthie said with all the enthusiasm she could muster, I am very happy this opportunity has arisen," she added. "If this is something you really want to do.

"Your voice sounds a little strained. Does the thought of my teaching disturb you in any way, sweetheart?" Ruth inquired.

"To be perfectly honest, Ruth, I am selfishly thinking about never eating lunch with you again and missing the hours I spend with you when I am not so busy with farm chores. At the same time, I am so proud that this brilliant woman has chosen me as her partner, and I want to do anything I can to encourage that fine mind. I think you should take it," Ruthie assured Ruth.

Ruth reached over and held Ruthie's hand as they headed to the farm. "I won't be away from you all that much, sweetheart. I'll still have breakfast with you in the morning and dinner with you at night. On the weekends, it will be our usual routine. And I am off every summer just when you need the most help. You do a great job providing for us, but it is time I helped a little bit more financially. I owe you so much," Ruth urged.

"Honey, you owe me nothing. It is *me* who owes you. Or is it *I* who owes you, English professor?" Ruthie laughed. "You have my blessing, Ruth, not that you need it. All I want is for you to be happy, and I can say it has been some time since I've seen you this excited. So, congratulations, dear. I am ready to share you with those young minds," Ruthie declared as she squeezed Ruth's hand.

Ruthie had to admit to herself that she felt, once again, a little undermined as the couple's financial base. She knew she was not Ruth's husband, but she always felt like the breadwinner in providing for Ruth, and there was satisfaction for her in that regard. She tried to show Ruth that her contribution to the farming effort was as important as her own by giving her every extra dollar that wasn't needed for their essentials. But of course, Ruth deserved a better life than the meager income from the farm. Ruth never complained about their tight finances, and that was the very reason Ruthie would let her pride disappear. It was a fact that many of the farmers in the county could not survive without the teacher salaries provided by their wives.

"I am so glad you approve, Ruthie, because I promised the principal I'd be in his office tomorrow at ten. He wants me to bring my teacher credentials and college transcript. I will feel so much more relaxed in our meeting if I know you are behind me. You know this provides a good reason for me to stay on with you at the farm. Also, we can eventually buy a second car and save for our retirement. You can't work on this farm forever, Ruthie. I worry about all the physically taxing work you do now," Ruth said.

After supper that night, Ruth went foraging through her trunk for her teaching credentials, diploma, and transcript. She laid them on the dining room table. Ruthie walked by as she placed the documents on the table. She asked if she could look at Ruth's diploma. Ruth showed her the diploma, which contained the words "summa cum laude." Ruthie knew what those words meant from her Latin classes in school. "Why don't you have this framed, my dear?" Ruthie inquired. "You should be so very proud of this diploma. It's one thing to go to one of the most prestigious women's colleges in the country and quite an additional accomplishment to graduate with highest honors. Let's get a frame for this and put it up near the bookshelves," Ruthie insisted.

"I don't think that is necessary. Most people know I went to Smith, and it seems like I am bragging by putting it on the wall," Ruth insisted.

"But why shouldn't you feel proud of this academic success? I am proud of you, and I'd like to sit in the rocking chair and look at it sometimes. Truth is, you should probably be teaching English at Smith and not just the Four Corners School District," Ruthie commented.

The next morning, Ruth was in Mr. Salter's office at the appointed time. Mr. Salter smiled as he looked over her transcript. "Well I knew from the Wednesday night Bible studies you have led at church that you were brilliant, but Phi Beta Kappa!" Mr. Salter exclaimed. "Have you thought about getting a master's or doctoral degree? You could be teaching in college, earning a much better salary than what we offer," Mr. Salter explained.

"What you say is probably true, Mr. Salter. I haven't had the money to seek another degree. When I graduated from Smith, I secured my teacher credentials from the Regents and headed back to Cooperstown to take care of my parents. Father was quite sick. I taught through World War II and on into the Korean conflict. Unfortunately, even though I was tenured, I was replaced last year by a veteran who was best friends with the principal in Cooperstown. I chose not to fight that injustice because, who was I compared to this veteran of the army with a family to support? Out of a job, I was invited to Four Corners to be a caretaker for Alma Stein. Losing my teaching job was tough but helping the Stein family seemed purposeful. I would be lying if I said this opportunity is not important to me, because it is," Ruth said.

"Well you have the job, Ruth. The salary is four thousand dollars a year paid in ten installments beginning September 15. I did call that Cooperstown principal to find out why you left. He explained about the veteran friend who had taught there before the wars. He said it was very difficult to let you go because the students enjoyed your classes and complained when you left. But his friend had a family to support in Cooperstown, so he had to let you go. By taking this job, you will also need to help the students put together the annual yearbook, and you may be asked to chaperone some dances from time to time. Will that be satisfactory?" Mr. Salter inquired.

"That would be fine, Mr. Salter," Ruth replied. Ruth thought about losing her former job in Cooperstown because the man had a family. Little did Mr. Salter know that she, too, now had a family, and it was time she did her part to make her household a little more financially sound.

"Then we will see you the Tuesday after Labor Day, and you can set up your room for the students to arrive the next day. We have a faculty meeting that Tuesday at 3:00 p.m.," Mr. Salter said. "Welcome aboard, Miss Packer." Mr. Salter beamed as he held out his hand for a handshake. He went on to explain he would have a contract for her drawn up by mid-August and would give her a telephone call to come in for the signing.

Ruth floated out of the school with racing thoughts about what novels she would use in her classes and how many compositions to assign in one semester. She drove home thinking about how much difference four thousand dollars a year would help the household. She would buy any food staples they needed, pay all the utilities, buy their clothes, and maybe treat herself once a month to a visit to the beauty parlor in the next town over. She would save for her and Ruthie's eventual retirement and maybe help them buy a new car. She was going to make a special celebratory supper tonight with Ruthie's favorite, pork chops and corn on the cob.

Ruth pulled into the driveway just as Ruthie was returning from the back pasture on the tractor. Ruth couldn't withhold her smile, and Ruthie knew instantly she had gotten the teaching position. As they walked into the garage together, Ruthie asked, "So when does Professor Packer begin her work? Congratulations, my dear," Ruthie shouted as she gave Ruth a big hug.

Chapter 14

Christmas 1953

It had been a good year for both Ruth and Ruthie. Ruth loved her teaching position as well as the extra income, and Ruthie had received an especially large end of the year dividend check from the cooperative to which she sold the farm's milk. They decided they wanted to make the Christmas season very special by decorating the house with a large Christmas tree and Christmas wreaths and inviting the Methodist women's Fellowship to their home on the second Saturday evening in December. After the Christmas Eve service, they would be alone to enjoy the remainder of the evening, and then go to the Packer farm for Christmas dinner.

Without Ruth's knowledge, Ruthie had arranged for the delivery of a used upright piano to their home the Friday night before they entertained the Methodist women. The piano had been lightly used and was part of an estate sale Ruthie had read about in the newspaper. Now Ruth could play Chopin or Christmas carols for the Methodist ladies the next night. She had arranged with Billy to get four men from the church to bring it to their door right after the supper hour, and Cindy had promised to make a big red ribbon with a note saying, "From Santa Claus." Having heard Ruth's exceptional piano playing skills at church, the men were eager to help surprise Ruth with this gift from Ruthie. Billy was glad Ruthie thought so much of his cousin Ruth to give her a piano for Christmas.

Ruthie had no idea that, at the very same time she was purchasing the piano, Ruth had put a new Zenith television on layaway as a Christmas gift for Ruthie. The cost of the TV had been $189, which Ruth had paid with her new teacher earnings, as well as the leftover egg money and blackberry sales. It was time for the two of them to start enjoying some shows together in the comfort of their home, where they could hold hands or cuddle on the sofa. Since they couldn't enjoy holding hands at the movie theater, why not have a private screening room? The television was to be delivered the morning before Christmas Eve.

When the piano arrived, Ruth was overcome with emotion, and the men delivering the surprise Christmas gift were happy when the tears of joy started rolling down her cheeks. "To whom do I owe a thank you for the best Christmas gift I've ever gotten?" she asked. "You should read the card attached to the ribbon," Billy suggested. As she gently pulled the card from the ribbon and opened it up she read "Santa Claus." Ruth smiled and knew who the Santa Claus in her life had been. She said nothing to Ruthie but turned toward Billy and the other men. "So, let me guess, you must be Santa's elves bringing a gift too large to fit down the chimney?" Everyone chuckled. "If that is the case, you'd better take a break and eat Santa's cookies with a glass of milk," Ruth insisted as she directed them to the kitchen table and grabbed the cookie jar and a gallon of milk.

"Well, maybe just one cookie for the road back to the North Pole," Billy replied, to which his cousin quipped, "Back to the North Pole? Don't you realize Four Corners is the North Pole! I've never been as cold in my life as I endured my first winter in this place. It was minus twenty this morning with a wind chill," Ruth grumbled. "Thank God Ruthie doesn't spare the coal or wood to keep us warm in this house," she added. "If she did, I'd have to go out in the barn and sleep on some straw next to the cows. It was a surprise to me how warm the barn can be in winter, until Ruthie explained how twenty-five cows could generate such body heat while also having the insulation from the haymow above them. Ruthie spoils them with the barn radio playing 'swing' music all during the milking, as well as pouring some molasses on their hay before she leaves the barn!" Ruth exclaimed.

"Well, I'll be." Billy laughed. "I swear you almost sound jealous of those cows, Ruth," he added. "Maybe now with this piano you play so well, you can convince Ruthie to come into the house more often for some even better music. It is pretty sad when a human being would rather spend more time with her cows than listening to Chopin live."

Ruthie had thought this conversation was headed in a bad direction, intimating that she hadn't been good enough to Ruth. But then she realized Ruth knew exactly what she was doing. She was throwing the whole Four Corners community off their love trail. The men would all go home and have a laugh about how Ruthie preferred time in the barn to time in the house with Ruth. And the wives would probably shake their heads and say something like, "Poor Ruthie, she'll never really change, will she!"

How little they knew, and the less the better! Her mind wandered back to late September last year when she went to the barn to see if Ruthie needed any help with the chores. Ruthie had smiled at Ruth and said, "Well, since you have your jeans on, I suppose it is time for me to show you the haymow and how I get the hay down to the cows," Ruthie said quite seriously.

Ruth obediently followed Ruthie up the ladder to the haymow, only to have Ruthie firmly pull her up the last wrung and into an area full of straw. After a long kiss and embrace, Ruthie said, "Straw can be used for a bed you know. Even baby Jesus had that experience."

With that comment, they both tumbled into a pile of straw and, once again, took pleasure in the profound love they had for one another with no fear anyone would find them. When they got up from the straw, they took turns pulling pieces of straw out of each other's hair while giggling like schoolgirls. Ruthie had then observed, "Let me never be accused of lacking spontaneity in the love department, my dear."

Ruth was brought back from her memory by Billy's request. "How about one quick Christmas carol before we go, so we can hear if Santa sent you a good piano."

Ruth sat down on the piano bench and played "Away in a Manger," glancing toward Ruthie with a smile.

The Christmas church season brought decoration night two weeks before Christmas when all the parishioners would gather to decorate the church after a 6:00 p.m. potluck supper. Of course, there was a special Christmas Eve service, followed by desserts and coffee and the arrival of Santa Claus in Fellowship Hall, bringing a box of assorted candies for every child in attendance.

With Ruth in her life, Ruthie enjoyed these events more than ever. Even driving the six miles to their Methodist church each Sunday was special for Ruthie as she chatted with Ruth about various members of their community.

On Sunday afternoons, after helping Ruth with the dishes, Ruthie often suggested they take a nap before she had to do the evening milking. They would ascend the stairs to their "Blue Heaven" and pull a warm quilt over their shoulders. With the warmth of the cover and Ruth's body, Ruthie was always asleep instantly. As she would listen to her love's steady breathing, Ruth would simply think to herself, *thank you, Lord, for this wonderful woman who works so hard and has chosen me to love.*

After a nice hour's nap, Ruthie would slide out from under the cover and head to the barn. It was time for the evening milking and the feeding of the Holsteins. These days, her faithful Jenny followed her out to the barn to keep an eye on things, especially all the barn cats Ruthie fed every night with milk. Ruthie had learned from her father to welcome feral cats into the barn to keep down the population of mice.

One night, shortly after Ruth had begun teaching, halfway through the milking, Ruthie felt dizzy and had a searing pain in the left portion of her chest. She placed the milk stool in the middle of the barn floor and sat down to catch her breath. Jenny seemed to sense something was wrong and went running to Ruthie, tilting her head as if to understand what was wrong with her owner. After a few minutes the pain eased, and Ruthie resumed her chores slowly. There was no need to rush. Ruth always kept their food warm until she came in from the barn.

When she returned from the barn that evening, the kitchen was warm and inviting. Ruth had the local radio station on, listening to swing music, while making some hot roast beef sandwiches and hot chocolate. Ruth looked at Ruthie as she entered the kitchen, and saw that Ruthie looked ashen. "Are you feeling okay, sweetheart?" Ruth inquired.

"Oh, I am just fine, my dear," Ruthie assured Ruth. "I might have been rushing just now out in the barn, and I think I might have pulled a muscle."

"Well, we'll have to see about that right after dinner. I think I have some Bengay in the medicine cabinet that should help," Ruth suggested.

"Not sure that will be necessary, but maybe a massage of the shoulders and back with that great smelling baby oil you got recently would loosen up my muscles a bit," Ruthie replied.

They sat at the kitchen table, said the usual blessing, and enjoyed Ruth's hot beef sandwiches, which included mashed potatoes and carrots on the side. Ruthie pushed back from the table and looked at Ruth to say, "Sometimes I don't know what I did to deserve you, Ruth. Another fine meal and a massage to look forward to."

Ruthie started to pick up the dishes for Ruth, but Ruth told her to put the dishes down, go upstairs and take a hot bath, and then the massage would do even more good to relieve her strained muscles. Ruthie did not fight her about this plan tonight. She'd had this pain before but had never spoken about it to anyone. She had sincerely prayed to God it would go away. But Ruthie knew the pain she was having was not sore muscles. She would have to find the time to get into Watertown to see a new doctor who had been recommended to her by Doc Ralph. He felt she should have a full cardiac examination, given her family history of stroke and heart failure. He wasn't happy that Ruthie's blood pressure was 180 over 100 that day. Doc Ralph had placed Ruthie on some medicine he referred to as "water pills" and pleaded with her to see the cardiologist as soon as she could.

She'd never told Ruth about her blood pressure reading or the new medication, which she kept in the barn. Trying to figure a reason for going into Watertown without Ruth would be the biggest hurdle. As the days went by, she convinced herself there was really nothing to her pain and she would simply stop whenever she was having this pain and wait for it to go away.

Chapter 15

The next ten years of their life together settled into the predictable yet sometimes hectic life of two fully employed women who also tried to serve their community. At the suggestion of Ruth once her teaching position began, Ruthie milked the cows after they had their breakfast together at about 6:00 a.m. Ruth was now the first one up in the morning, brewing coffee and preparing the breakfast fare, which both women had agreed needed to become somewhat lighter in content and calories, as they both stared directly into the face of middle age. In the summer, the breakfast was almost always scrambled eggs, bacon, and toast with one of the jams Ruth made, along with orange juice and coffee. In the winter, Ruth made oatmeal, replete with raisins and walnuts, with just a touch of brown sugar on top.

Ruth always made lunch for herself and Ruthie right after breakfast. Lunch for Ruthie was left in the refrigerator. After quickly doing the dishes, Ruth would dash upstairs and get dressed for school as Ruthie headed to the barn. By 7:00 a.m., Ruth was on her way to school, and Ruthie was milking the cows. Ruthie easily adjusted to sleeping in an hour longer in the morning and noted she did better completing her farm chores on a full breakfast.

In the summertime, when Ruth was home from her school duties, their lives returned to the routine they had known before Ruth got the teaching position. Ruth was busier than ever in the summers, tending to the garden, canning, cooking for the extra farmhands who helped harvest the crops on the Stein farm, and tending to the chickens and egg collection, which Ruthie had taken over in the school year months. Ruth never minded the extra summer duties because it was a change of pace from trying to open students' young minds to the world beyond Four Corners.

They attended church every Sunday together and, between the two of them, held almost every position in the church, including trustee. Because of her practical understanding of the appropriate costs for running a church, all the men asked Ruthie to join them on the Board of Trustees in 1956. She was the first woman ever to be appointed to this trusted position in their church. Both assumed different offices in the Women's Fellowship.

Ruth taught the adult Bible study class before church, rushing off from that obligation to the piano, where she continued to play for the Sunday services. Based on her great talent teaching the adult Sunday School class and the large number of adults who attended it, the pastor even suggested she might consider becoming a lay preacher, who could fill in on Sundays for surrounding preachers who were taking vacation or ill. When he suggested this, Ruth thanked him politely but declined, saying, "With my teaching and my summer farm duties, as well as my service already to this church in other assignments, my time is all taken."

Ruth also pointed out she would prefer to worship with her own congregation every Sunday. When the congregation heard the pastor had made the lay preacher position suggestion, they were amazed a woman had been asked to be a lay preacher. Although ordination of women as full-time pastors was now possible in the Methodist Church, it was exceptionally rare when a woman climbed into the pulpit. It was a fine compliment to Ruth's extraordinary mind.

Their social life together during this time was mostly watching television and going to church celebrations. And when their birthdays arrived, they would make a special date to go into Watertown by themselves for a movie and a meal at the Crystal Restaurant. They faithfully watched *The Ed Sullivan Show* as he paraded the newest comics and singing sensations to his stage, from Elvis Presley in the 1950s to the Beatles in the 1960s.

During the 1959–1960 school year, Ruth met the new girl's physical education teacher, June. She and June hit it off immediately and often shared their lunches in the faculty lounge at noontime. June reminded Ruth of Ruthie, except that June was more outspoken than Ruthie and didn't mind offending her fellow teachers' sensibilities if the occasion called for it. June was medium height and had black hair and brown eyes but seemed as physically powerful as Ruthie. It was obvious she practiced what she preached when it came to physical education. June was Italian and had graduated from Buffalo University. She came from a working-class family and was the first woman in her family to graduate from college. June had applied for numerous teaching positions but decided to move some distance from her large family in Buffalo, so she could have "the freedom to be myself," accepting the position at Four Corners School District. Ruth and June were the only unmarried teachers at the high school.

One afternoon, about two months after she had joined the high school faculty, June traveled to Ruth's classroom after the students had left for the day. She stared through the window at this distinguished-looking woman with salt-and-pepper hair and gently tapped on the window. Ruth looked up and saw June. She put down her glasses, smiled, and waved at June to come in her classroom. "Well, to what do I owe this honor of your presence?" Ruth began. "Can't be you have an out-of-control young lady and need advice on how to handle her. I can well imagine you are fully capable of taking care of those matters yourself by requiring thirty laps around the gym or forty sit-ups in a minute." Ruth laughed.

June made sure the door was closed before she replied. "Forgive me for being impertinent, Ruth, but I need to ask you something of a personal nature. You mentioned you lived on a farm with another woman and that she does all the farm work. That is just so unusual I wanted to know more," June inquired.

Ruth's heart picked up its pace considerably as she intently considered the eyes of her lunch mate. "Yes, it is true I live with Ruthie on her farm, and I admit that it is quite unusual for a woman to have farming as her vocation. But Ruthie is an amazing woman and not just some 'hick from the sticks.' She graduated top of her high school class with an honors Regents Diploma, and had she been given the opportunity, I am certain she would have been accepted at Cornell for the veterinarian program. She would have been the best vet you could hire. She loves animals and appears to have a special way of relating to them," Ruth answered.

"I hear much affection in your voice when you talk about Ruthie. How amazing that both of you have the same first name. How did this all happen that the two of you began living together, if I may ask?" June inquired.

Ruth wanted to proceed with caution in answering June's very personal inquiries. "Well, Ruthie's mother broke her hip and became an invalid. My cousin Billy lived next door to Ruthie, and they were fast friends. I was out of a teaching position just then, and he wondered if I might consider working for Ruthie as she tried to maintain the farm and take care of her mother. I had very briefly met Ruthie once before at a large Packer family reunion and knew, if Ruthie was my cousin Billy's best friend, she was a good woman. So, I agreed to help and moved into the farmhouse to take care of Alma Stein, as well as assuming some housekeeping duties to help Ruthie. We got along just famously, and I am still there. Is there anything else you want to ask me, June?" Ruth asked, raising one eyebrow and smiling.

"I am sorry," June began. "Am I being too personal and forward? If so, forgive me. I guess it is just part of my working-class Italian nature to ask too many questions of people. You probably don't know what it is like to come from a large Italian family, where everyone is into everyone else's business. As you know, that is why I moved some distance away from my old neighborhood," June said.

"It's okay to ask me questions. If we are going to be friends, it is important to know all the pertinent facts about each other's life. You are not the only one who has asked too many questions of people. Before I went off to Smith, my mother did the best she could to remind me that proper young ladies don't ask a lot of questions about another's personal life. 'Rather,' she used to say, 'wait for them to voluntarily reveal the particulars of their life, and in time, if you become good friends, you'll know just about everything'. I haven't always taken my mother's advice; believe me! I find myself too inquisitive about people. I let my heart take over my mouth instead of engaging my brain." Ruth laughed. "Now it is my turn to ask a question, and we will take it from there. Have you ever lived with another woman?" Ruth boldly inquired.

June smiled back at Ruth, whom she hoped would become her very dear friend, and said, "As a matter of fact, I have, Ruth. Her name was Susie, and we met at college. The last year of our studies we got an apartment together in Buffalo, and we were both thankful to get out of those crazy dormitories, where no one ever has any privacy at all. I trust my judgment in assuming you are the type of friend who knows what it means to keep one's confidence, Ruth. Am I right about that?" June asked Ruth, while displaying a look of concern on her face.

"Unless you are about to tell me you have murdered someone, I can assure you that, when a friend asks me to stay silent about something they have told me, I do just that. So, what do you want to tell me?" Ruth asked.

"Well, I was in love with Susie, and I thought she loved me. Our relationship began the last semester of our junior year, and that is why we got the apartment together our senior year. We were trying to figure out that senior year how we could stay together and be teaching in different locations. I thought it was worth the effort, at least to try and locate physical education positions near one another. However, as May approached, and we were three weeks from graduation, Susie came back from classes one afternoon and told me she didn't think our type of relationship was good for our teaching profession. When

I asked her exactly what she was trying to tell me, she said she wanted to break off our contact with one another and have the freedom to date men again. I can't tell you how shocked I was. It was Susie who made the overtures to me to be intimate with her, and I thought we were good together as we moved deeper into our physical relationship. This was another reason, maybe the real reason, I moved so far away from Buffalo. I knew if I stayed in the locale, all the places we had gone together that last year of college would remind me of her," June explained as she averted her eyes from Ruth and stared out the classroom windows.

Ruth could see that this experience had really left June quite broken and confused, somewhat like she herself had felt in her experimentation with Henrietta at Smith. She wanted to make June feel a little better about the situation, and she guessed June had never really discussed this breakup with anyone before. She didn't wait too long to respond because she did not want June to feel as if she had done something immoral and staying silent for very long might lead her to that conclusion.

Ruth spoke up quickly but quietly in response to June's anguish and confusion. "Look, June, Susie is the loser here. And I am so sorry this had to happen to you. Something similar happened to me when I was in college, and I left college wondering who I was when it came to the issue of physical relationships. I had dated men. I dated men after I graduated from Smith and lived in Cooperstown, but I never let a few dates turn into sex. I knew I was attracted to women, and while I enjoyed the companionship of a man for dinner out and a movie, going to bed with them was nothing I wanted. All my confusion about who I was and what I wanted out of life in the love department cleared up the first time I fully laid eyes on Ruthie. I can only tell you that, when I saw her, our eyes met, and I was just thunderstruck. I also sensed she felt the same way. The kindest, loving smile came over Ruthie's face, and that was it for me. She is the first and only woman with whom I have really been intimate, and so it was for her as well."

June had been listening so intently to Ruth that she realized she had been gripping the side of her chair to the point her fingers ached. "Ruth, you have no idea how relieved I feel right this minute. Finally, somebody I know and highly respect knows who I really am. I've looked up to you from the day I arrived at this school. I knew you were brilliant because of Smith, and I knew you were kind because of what the students said about you. You seemed to have a confidence about yourself I rarely see in other women."

"If I have that confidence as you say, June, it is only because I am almost twice your age and have years of experience living independently from society's expectations of who I should be. You are just beginning your life, my dear, and there is no doubt in my mind whatsoever that there is someone out there just waiting for you to walk into her life. Finding someone may seem impossible at times, but then the strangest combination of factors can end up tossing you into the arms of your life companion," Ruth assured June.

"I hope I am as lucky as you, Ruth. This Ruthie must be some kind of woman to have taken off the market a gorgeous woman like you!" June replied.

"I don't know about the gorgeous part as it concerns me, but Ruthie is quite a woman. She is the type of person you can rely upon no matter what calamity you may be facing. She will take charge of what might seem to be an insolvable problem and make it all better. We didn't jump into bed together right away. Our love grew during the six months I took care of her invalid mother. Our love was tested during that time in many ways. Some time, I will tell you all about that. I think it would be very nice for you to come to our farm and meet Ruthie. I think I can speak for both of us that your friendship would be a welcome relief from our women friends from church. It would be good for us to get a younger perspective of love between two women. Does that sound like a possibility?" Ruth asked.

June quickly accepted that invitation, and before long, she was having dinner at Ruth and Ruthie's home at least twice a month. June even got snowed in at the farmhouse one Friday night and was unable to drive back to her apartment before Monday morning. During that time, she had helped Ruthie with some of the farm chores and enjoyed learning about all the farm animals. It was amazing how cozy and warm the barn could be even though a blizzard raged outside. June could see how intelligent and organized Ruthie was about her farm operation and how physically powerful Ruthie could be in dispatching forty-pound bales about the barn with little effort. During that same weekend, she tasted Ruth's amazing cooking, as well as devoured Ruth's baked goods. She could see how in love the two women appeared to be as they held hands while watching TV and she never heard them argue. If only she could find a life of love with another woman.

Some things had changed at the Stein farmhouse as the decade of the sixties descended upon Ruth and Ruthie. Ruth seemed to be more aware of these changes than Ruthie. They remained kind and considerate of one another, but their intimacy in bed had tapered off considerably. Ruthie seemed exhausted most of the time, and Ruth soon grew tired of trying to convince Ruthie they needed to reignite the passion they had experienced. Ruthie was resistant to taking any vacations and leaving her cows to hired hands, and when Ruth suggested Billy might oversee a week or so of milking, Ruthie was firm in her conviction that it was too much to ask of Billy. It did occur to Ruth that Ruthie was beginning menopause and that these changing hormones, which sometimes left Ruthie sweating in the middle of the night and unable to sleep, were certainly affecting a desire to cuddle and be affectionate. Ruth let herself be satisfied with the good night kiss Ruthie gave her every night as they crawled in bed and the secure feeling of Ruthie holding her hand as they slept.

Both women were intently focused on their assigned vocations, and church or school activities often intruded on any spare time they might find for cuddling and relaxing.

One morning as she was driving to school, Ruth realized that the two companions had long ago ceased reading the *Upper Room* together. While Sunday church remained a constant in their lives, and they always said grace before meals, they shared little about their faith with one another anymore. Early in their relationship, they had often discussed their faith and their purpose on earth. Ruth had long thought that shared spiritual concerns were the glue that held two people together, no matter what perils they faced. There was an uneasiness falling upon their relationship, and Ruth didn't like it.

Ruth also didn't like the way she had begun enjoying June's company a little too much. She had to admit to herself that she was attracted to June, and she knew June was attracted to her, as evidenced by constant little compliments June was throwing her way when they were out of earshot of others. June was dating a woman in Watertown but talked little of making it a permanent arrangement.

Chapter 16

March 15, 1964

As soon as Ruth pulled into the driveway from school, she knew something was wrong. Jenny ran to the car and was barking furiously. When Ruth stepped out of the auto, Jenny jumped up on Ruth and started whining.

"What's wrong, girl?" Ruth pleaded.

Jenny turned, ran toward the barn, and then stopped to make sure Ruth was following her. She then continued running to the side barn door with Ruth right behind. Once inside the barn, Jenny led Ruth to Ruthie, lying in a heap on the concrete barn floor below the haymow trapdoor. Ruthie was moaning in pain.

"Oh my God. Ruthie, what happened?" Ruth shouted as she ran to Ruthie and tried to put Ruthie's head in her lap.

Ruthie explained that, as she was getting some hay from the loft, she had fallen through the trapdoor onto the concrete, and she couldn't seem to move. She had been on the barn floor for about an hour. Ruth took off her coat and sweater, wadding up the sweater as a pillow for Ruthie's head. She then placed her winter coat over Ruthie's body to try and prevent shock. "Thank God you put a phone in the barn. I am calling Doc Ralph, Billy, and an ambulance. I'll be right back. Jenny, lay right next to your mommy and take care of her until I get back," Ruth instructed the faithful dog.

Ruth ran to the barn phone and called Billy and Doc Ralph.

She was deeply concerned as she contemplated the possible injuries Ruthie had sustained and felt badly that Ruthie had been lying on that cold barn floor for an hour. Thank God for Jenny, who no doubt had stayed by Ruthie's side until she'd heard the car coming in the driveway. Jenny was the smartest dog Ruth had ever seen. Ruth and Ruthie had trained Jenny to get one of them when the other needed help and stay behind when needed. She had certainly done that today.

She ran back to Ruthie's side and grabbed her hand. Ruthie tried to be brave but started to cry. "How did I let this happen? What will become of us?" Ruthie sobbed.

Ruth kissed her on the forehead. "We will be fine, Ruthie. We will figure it all out. And remember, I have a good job now. It's my time to take care of you. We will figure it out. We will figure it out," Ruth kept repeating as she stroked Ruthie's forehead.

When Billy arrived with the doctor, Billy knelt by Ruthie with a look of intense concern and took her other hand as the doctor carefully manipulated her back and legs. When he heard how she had fallen from the hayloft, Billy asked, "Did this have to do with that dizziness you experienced during the haying season? You certainly are not clumsy. You must have passed out up there."

Ruth was at a loss for words as she stared at her cousin and then Ruthie. "What dizziness are you talking about? I didn't know she was having any dizziness," Ruth stated.

Billy was in trouble now with Ruthie, but if that was the price for saving her life by revealing symptoms of something even more ominous than the fall, so be it. "Well, Ruthie didn't want you to worry about her. But one day when we were baling hay, she got real dizzy and had to stop driving the tractor. She told me it was just the heat—that this had happened to her before, and she'd be fine after some water and a five-minute rest."

She didn't want to upset Ruthie any more right now, but Ruth was hurt that Ruthie had kept this health problem to herself. Ruthie did not have the best family medical history, with her father dying from a stroke at age fifty-eight, and her mother recently dying of congestive heart failure. She didn't want to think about life without Ruthie. She had believed that, after twelve years together, she and Ruthie told each other everything. They would talk about this lapse in sharing the good and the bad after this immediate crisis was resolved.

Doc Ralph had preliminarily assessed that Ruthie had broken her pelvis in the fall. She would need to be taken by ambulance to Watertown for x-rays and hospitalization. Ruthie, still writhing in pain, asked Doc Ralph how long he thought she would be out of commission for her farm chores.

"Can't rightly say, my dear, until we know what the x-rays tell us. But you do need to know that you have some serious injuries here, and it is unlikely you will be tending any cows anytime soon," Doc replied.

Tears started streaming down her cheeks even faster when Ruthie heard this unwelcome appraisal of her broken body. Billy and Ruth knew Ruthie was inconsolable, but each tried their best to comfort her.

"Look at me, Ruthie," Billy insisted. "You are not to worry about your chores. They will all be done or arranged by the Packer family. You can count on it. After all you have done for the whole family, especially for my cousin here, it is time we paid back that great debt." He squeezed Ruthie's hand to reassure her.

Ruth followed Billy's reassurances with her own. "Ruthie, haven't we always thanked the good Lord every morning for all our blessings? We've been deeply blessed, and with God's help, we will pull through. We were Depression kids and learned from our parents to never give up and to know that, somehow, we'd figure how to get by. We will get this all figured out once you are on the mend." Ruth kissed Ruthie's hand and continued to hold it as Billy went looking for the ambulance.

Once Ruthie was in the ambulance, Ruth got into Billy's car and followed the ambulance into Watertown. Doc Ralph had phoned ahead to the hospital from the Stein barn and told the hospital staff they should locate a doctor prepared to do orthopedic surgery. Doc Ralph, now into his mid-eighties but still spritely, rode in the ambulance with Ruthie. As Billy and Ruth headed to the hospital, Billy looked over at Ruth and saw tears streaming down her cheeks. He grabbed his cousin's hand. "Ruthie will be fine, Ruth. She is such a strong woman. She can get past any obstacle." Ruth remained silent. "You know we rarely are alone to talk about things, but you really love Ruthie, don't you?"

Ruth wanted to tell the whole story of her love for Ruthie, but she knew Ruthie wouldn't want that, and she had to respect Ruthie's privacy. She suspected that Billy and Cindy had more than once privately discussed the depth of her relationship with Ruthie. "Well, who doesn't love Ruthie!" Ruth affirmed. "Of course, I love her."

Billy wanted his cousin to understand he was happy they had a "special friendship." He pressed on. "Yes, it is true everybody loves Ruthie. But you are in love with one another, aren't you?" Billy persisted.

"Why would you ask that?" Ruth responded.

"Look, cousin, I want you to know that, if the answer to my question is yes, I am very happy for you both. In fact, I would be relieved to know that you have made a lifelong commitment to one another. This conversation never leaves this car, even to Cindy. You know I can keep secrets. I didn't tell you about Ruthie's dizziness that Ruthie made me swear not to tell you," Billy pointed out. "I look at life a little differently than most. I want Ruthie to be happy, and she has been the happiest I have ever seen her since you came into her life," Billy added.

Ruth wiped her eyes and told Billy, "You are right. We are in love with one another. I have never told anyone. It would not be good if people knew that we are a couple like you and Cindy. I would no doubt lose my teaching position, which Ruthie and I are going to need more than ever now. But I am glad you know. I may need your advice on a lot of things in the weeks ahead." Ruth sighed.

"Anything you need, you just ask. And may I say Ruthie chose an attractive, brilliant, and kind woman to spend her life with," Billy said as he turned to his cousin and smiled.

As they arrived at the hospital, Ruthie was taken immediately to the x-ray room. Billy knew the routine well, since he had been through this with Ruthie when Mrs. Stein broke her hip.

It didn't take as long this time to hear about the extent of Ruthie's injuries. The orthopedic surgeon explained that Ruthie had broken her right hip, as well as her pelvis. She would need at least three weeks in the hospital, extensive rehabilitation, and no heavy physical work for at least six months. They also discovered Ruthie had very high blood pressure and had given her some medication to stabilize it. It was explained that she was still waking up from the hip procedure, but the nurse would come and get them when she was awake.

Billy asked the doctor if he would be giving this news to Ruthie when she awoke. He introduced himself as Ruthie's next-door neighbor and Ruth as Ruthie's housemate. The doctor shook both their hands and reassured them both that Ruthie would survive her injuries and that she was lucky she hadn't fallen headfirst onto the concrete floor.

About fifteen minutes later, the nurse came for them and said Ruthie could be seen for just a few minutes. Billy insisted Ruth go in the room without him and sat back down in the waiting room. Ruth smiled at him and quietly replied, "Thank you."

As Ruth entered the room, she was shocked to see Ruthie all bandaged and so vulnerable, but she kept her composure as she walked to the side of the bed and took Ruthie's hand. She looked about the room and into the hallway. Seeing no one, she bent over the bed and kissed Ruthie on the lips.

Ruthie smiled. She remained quiet as Ruth squeezed her hand. Ruthie finally said, "I suppose the doctor has given you the bad news. This surely is my Ides of March. I won't be of much use to you now for a few weeks, dear. You'd be better off on your own, Ruth," Ruthie grumbled.

"What an absurd thing for you to say," Ruth replied in a scolding voice. "Maybe we never got to say, 'for better or worse, in sickness and in health' in front of a whole bunch of people, but isn't that what we've always promised one another?"

Ruthie continued to look directly into the eyes of the woman she had always thought deserved someone better than herself to be her lifetime companion. "You need to know, Ruth, that I not only love you but that I always took pride in being able to provide you with a home. It made me feel better about myself than I had ever felt in my life. And, now this happens. I can't ask you to look after an invalid, especially with your teaching job and all," Ruthie countered.

"Now you look here, Ruthie. You don't have to ask me to take care of you, because I have been taking care of you since we met. Isn't that true? Or are you saying that the work you do on the farm and its income is more important than my cooking, cleaning, and teaching?" Ruth replied in a stern voice.

Ruthie was speechless. Ruth had never talked to her like this before. Had Ruth believed these past twelve years that her companion had not valued her contribution to the success of the farming endeavor? "Oh, no, no, no, honey. Even before you got that teaching position, I thought of you as like a wife who made the success of the farm possible with all you did for us," Ruthie said. "You made my life worth living, and I know how hard you've worked doing all the housekeeping duties, taking care of the chickens, putting in the vegetable garden, canning and freezing vegetables and fruits, washing all the clothes, dusting and cleaning the house, entertaining the Methodist women, all you do for the church, cooking, baking. In fact, it tires me out to lie here and think about all you did and continue to do on the farm, especially now that you teach as well. I am sorry if I have taken you for granted." Ruthie choked out her words as the tears began.

Ruth knew she had been uncharacteristically stern with Ruthie, but she knew Ruthie's stubbornness about work and her reluctance to ask for help. That would all have to change now. She had let Ruthie take the lead in most financial matters, but it was time for her to take over in that respect, at least in the year ahead. "Ruthie, I love you. That is all you must remember. It is time for me to step up and help us get through this little setback. I need to return to the farm with Billy now, but I will stop in to see you after my school day is done. Until then, you need to sleep all you can and do everything the nurses and doctors tell you to do. The best thing you can do for me is to get well enough to come home to me." With those words, seeing no one in the hallway, Ruth kissed Ruthie's lips again and exited the room.

As Ruth and Billy drove back to Four Corners, they discussed the alternatives for Ruthie's future. "You know, Billy, what this all means, don't you? Ruthie cannot farm any more. These fractures and high blood pressure won't allow her to do heavy physical work. I am mad at myself for not recognizing her high blood pressure problem. She has seemed much more fatigued in recent months and goes straight to bed after supper these days."

"Don't feel guilty, Ruth. I'm the one who kept her confidence and didn't tell you. She had been feeling dizzy. I should have given her an alternative of either going to Doc Ralph and getting a checkup within the week or I would tell you about the dizziness. Just think how guilty I feel! I bet you a sawbuck that she got dizzy up there in the mow and tumbled right down onto the concrete floor," Billy added.

"While it seems strange to say, this accident may have been a blessing in disguise. Ruthie is forty-four. In my mind, that is too old for a lone woman to be farming when she had a father who died at fifty-eight from a stroke. She has done hard physical work for thirty years, outworking her dad as soon as she hit her teen years. That's enough. I can support the two of us now on my salary. Ruthie won't want to hear about that, but it is the truth. In fact, I thought as I drove home from school today, I should plan a dinner for Saturday, inviting you and Cindy to help Ruthie and I celebrate the promotion I just received today," Ruth mentioned as she stared out the car window.

"My goodness, Ruth. What is the promotion?" Billy asked with excitement in his voice.

"Well, Mr. Salter called me into his office to tell me Mr. Browne was suddenly retiring due to heart problems and that he wanted me to replace him as vice principal," Ruth replied in a very matter-of-fact tone of voice.

"Vice principal! That's a first isn't it? I've never heard of a woman holding a position like that anywhere! My cousin the vice principal, congratulations!" Billy said enthusiastically.

"Thanks. But the best thing about it is that I get a two thousand dollar a year raise. I will still have to teach two English classes a day, but most of the time I will be handling discipline cases and counseling students about their plans after high school. I'll be busy for sure," Ruth explained. "As I was sitting in the waiting room after being told the extent of Ruthie's injuries, I knew how serendipitous my promotion was as it arrived the very day Ruthie's fortunes at farming would come to an end," Ruth mused.

Billy took a moment to respond as they drove along. "Ruth, I do believe God works in mysterious ways, but don't discount your own academic excellence in getting this promotion. Cindy's niece Marilyn took your English class as you know. Marilyn just went on and on about how fabulous you are as a teacher and how you managed to keep control of your class without being mean or sarcastic. Don't think for a minute that Mr. Salter hasn't heard those same compliments. And then there's your Smith credentials, with 'summa cum laude' written on that diploma. I don't think those factors should be overlooked. God's blessing to you was giving you that amazing brain, and you used that talent," Billy insisted. "Did you tell Ruthie about this promotion when you went in to see her?"

"No, I didn't. I thought that it would be best to tell her after the extent of her injury has really sunk in. I will tell her when I stop by after school tomorrow. Hopefully it will relieve some of her anxiety about our finances. If I had my way, Ruthie would sell that farm to you, and we would either buy a small one-story home or rent an apartment. Rent is only about a hundred to a hundred twenty-five dollars around here when you can find some place," Ruth said in a subdued voice. "Moving off that farm is the last thing she will want to do and being dependent on me financially will crush her sense of self-worth," Ruth added.

"Yes, I don't envy you," Billy admitted. "She is very sweet when she is in control, but stubborn as heck when she is not. I think that is partly true because she had to be so emotionally strong from early on in her childhood. Alma wasn't always happy and sometimes not very supportive of her daughter, as you know. Thank God, her father doted on her, but he always deferred to Alma when it came to parenting. I cannot begin to tell you how crushed Ruthie was when her father died in 1950 when she was just thirty. I wanted her to marry me, so she wouldn't feel so all alone in the world with Alma. But now I know why that would never happen. What is it everybody is saying at church these days, 'God has a reason for everything that happens'?"

"Well, I don't believe that completely," Ruth answered. "I think God gives us free choice, and as Jesus said, 'The rain falls on the just and unjust alike.' It is up to us to discover and create the upside to our misfortune," Ruth asserted.

"You know I would be interested in buying the farm. Maybe we could work out some deal as part of the sale of the farm for the two of you to remain in the farmhouse, at least until you can find someplace else you would want to live." Billy suggested.

"Thanks for that offer, Billy. It would all have to be agreed upon with Ruthie. While staying in the farmhouse until her recuperation is complete would alleviate some of the stress of all these changes to her life, she cannot remain on that farm for the rest of her life. She would be wandering out to the barn and trying to help with chores when it is the last thing she should be doing. I know if we stayed in the farmhouse, she would insist on paying you rent, as would I," Ruth replied.

They arrived at the farm about 1:00 a.m., and after saying good night to her cousin, Ruth went in search of the ever-faithful Jenny. She was sleeping in the garage just outside the kitchen door and was overjoyed to see Ruth. "I bet you are starved, sweet girl," Ruth said. "Your second mom was thoughtless tonight and forgot to mention to someone that you needed to be fed. But I will try to make up for it."

Jenny turned her head from side to side, trying to understand what Ruth was saying. She followed Ruth into the kitchen but lay down facing the back door, listening intently. Ruth knew Jenny thought Ruthie would be following them into the kitchen soon.

Ruth found leftover pot roast in the refrigerator. She made herself a small sandwich but mixed up most of the meat with Jenny's kibble and gave it to the hungry dog. "You and I are going to be by ourselves tonight, Jenny. It will be strange without your buddy, but I guess we will have to manage," Ruth told Jenny.

Ruth slowly ate her sandwich with a glass of milk, thinking about how hard it would be to talk to Ruthie about her new physical limitations and moving away from farming duties. She wasn't so sure Ruthie could see herself being primarily financially supported by Ruth. But this was something Ruth wanted to do, and she would find the right words to convince Ruthie she needed to take better care of herself by moving away from such taxing physical work.

Ruth slowly got undressed for bed as Jenny stared at her and then the bedroom door, no doubt still expecting Ruthie to show up for bed. Ruth crawled into bed completely exhausted. As Jenny stared at her, Ruth said, while patting the side of the bed where Ruthie usually slept, "Come on up, girl, and curl up next to me. We can comfort one another."

Jenny did not hesitate and jumped up on the bed, giving Ruth a couple of licks on the face before settling into Ruthie's spot with her head on Ruthie's pillow.

The next morning, Ruth arrived at school on time, despite only four hours of sleep. She got up earlier than usual to review her lesson plans for school as she drank three large cups of coffee and ate two pieces of toast. She was in her office when Principal Salter appeared at the doorway. "I thought you might be taking a personal day today? All of Four Corners has heard about your housemate's terrible fall."

"Yes, I found Ruthie on the barn floor when I arrived home from school late yesterday afternoon. The whole experience for all of us was traumatic. Her cousin Billy was with me throughout the whole emergency response and her admission to the hospital. I told Ruthie I would stop by the hospital after school. She will be in the hospital for three weeks, and there is nothing I could do to help the medical personnel. My responsibilities are here right now, and I want to do a good job as your vice principal," Ruthie replied.

"I am glad you are here, but please, if you need to leave during any day, I approve. In all the years you've worked in this district, you have never taken a sick day or a personal day. If you need one or more days, take them, and let me know how Ruthie's doing. In my conversations with her at church, I have found her to be very well spoken, and many have mentioned she was valedictorian of her class. No wonder you get along so well. I'm sure Ruthie appreciates your fine mind. Too bad she never got to go to college like you," Mr. Salter observed.

"Yes, that is too bad. She would have been a great veterinarian with her way with animals. And at forty-four, she should not be doing the hard-physical work she does. Thanks for your concern, and I will keep you apprised of her condition," Ruth replied, before turning her eyes back to her lesson plans. She sensed Principal Slater knew exactly the status of her relationship with Ruthie. It did not seem to matter to him, and she was grateful he was one of the more progressive minds in Four Corners.

All during that school day, Ruth tried to rehearse the conversation she would need to have with Ruthie. She did not look forward to telling her their lives would have to change drastically. When she got to the hospital at about 4:00 p.m., no one was in the room with Ruthie. It appeared to her that Ruthie was sound asleep, but when she went to the side of the bed, Ruthie opened her eyes and smiled.

"How's the pain today?" Ruth asked as she knelt to kiss her on the forehead. "Let me bring this chair next to the side of the bed so we can have a nice, long chat," Ruth said before Ruthie had a chance to speak.

"I guess my pain has eased with the morphine they are giving me today. They say they will be starting me on something called Percodan tomorrow for pain relief. I've been sleeping most of today waiting for your visit," Ruthie said.

"I didn't take the day off from school because I thought I might need the day or days of personal leave when you are released from the hospital," Ruth explained. "I sure missed you last night, and so did your faithful dog, who kept waiting for you to come home. It was so sad. I tried not to cry."

"Well don't think I didn't miss you and Jenny. Off and on during the night and again today, I kept thinking about how my clumsiness has plummeted us into this mess. I am trying to figure out a way forward. I guess maybe I will ask Billy if he can find some hired hands to do the chores until I am back doing them myself. It will take a big chunk out of our budget, but it will just have to be done." Ruthie sighed.

Now was the time Ruth had dreaded. The reality of their situation had to be brought to light. She would also let Ruthie know of her new vice principal position and the added pay. She knew this would not be enough to convince her companion to give up what she had been doing steadily for well over thirty years. There was nothing to do but plow ahead with the truth.

"Ruthie, the doctor did tell you about the extent of your injuries last night, did he not?"

"Yes. I know I took a bad fall and will need to be in this hospital for three weeks. I expect that will give me enough time to recover and get back out to the barn, maybe with the help of a couple hired hands. You know I am tough, Ruth, and I am no wimp when it comes to pain. All this talk of me lying around in the house for months is just nonsense," Ruthie confidently replied.

"No, Ruthie, you are wrong. Breaking your pelvis and right hip is very serious to say the least. It will take several months before you can be lifting anything heavy or squatting on a milk stool to milk the cows. Furthermore, I don't want you to do those chores ever again. You turned forty-four the first of this month, and you have been doing this hard work since your father would first let you into the barn. It is time to make a different life with me. God blessed us yesterday. I was coming home yesterday afternoon to tell you Mr. Salter had offered me the vice principal's position with a two thousand dollar a year raise. With this added income, we can survive just fine. My contract with the school district provides for annual merit pay increases. We will need to find something different for you to do. I don't expect you to cook and clean. Surely God has something else he wants you to do with your life," Ruth said.

Ruthie silently stared at Ruth and didn't know quite what to say. She was glad Ruth had gotten this well-deserved promotion, but next to Ruth's love, the farm was all she wanted in life, and she knew she was good at farming. What else could she do for work in Four Corners? She had no college education, nor had she gone to business school to learn secretarial skills. Ruthie finally gained her composure and began to speak. "I am so proud of you for your promotion, my dear. That is a huge compliment and a huge salary increase. But what am I to do? Seems like there is nothing for me to do. God knows, I would try to keep house for us, but I'd never do it as well as you do. There would be hours I would just be mourning the loss of your companionship. What will happen to the Stein farm? Where will we live?" Ruthie started to cry.

Ruth held Ruthie's hand very tightly and wiped the tears from Ruthie's cheeks. "I know this is so much for you to take in all at one time, sweetheart. I wish things could be different, but they aren't. You are facing the realities of aging when you have a tough physical vocation and can no longer keep up the pace. You've always wanted to be the complete provider. You've never wanted anyone to help you out.

Changing your outlook on life will take time. Remember last night when I told you all you needed to focus on right now is my love for you and your own healing? Nothing's changed since last night. Your fall may be the tonic we need to move on to a new adventure together. Do you realize we have been together for twelve years, and we have never taken a vacation because of those cows?! Honestly, sometimes I think that farm has impeded our love life in the last few years. Since I have summers off, maybe we can do some traveling. There is so much right in this very state I'd love to show you. We might even take a trip to New York City later this summer. The world's fair will be there. Maybe we could get you well enough to go!" Ruth smiled as she thought about this possibility.

Ruthie knew Ruth did not intend to make her feel badly about their relationship but being told their love life was not satisfactory was of real concern to her. How would it be now that she was just a bundle of bandages and sleeping a lot of the time because of painkillers? She had to admit that, in recent years, their physical contact had been reduced to hand-holding on the couch and a kiss before Ruth went off to work in the morning. Why hadn't they talked about the mundane state of their physical affection?

"But what about the farm? Who will work it if I don't? Are you asking me to sell it? If I do, we would need to move to another home or apartment rental. I suppose we could sell off the acreage, farm equipment, cows, and barn and keep the house," Ruthie sadly proposed.

"There is nothing we need to decide this minute. You need time to think about what you want for a home and time to absorb the fact you cannot do the rugged job of dairy farming after these injuries. When an event like your fall occurs in our lives, we often waste too much time bemoaning the inevitable instead of considering all the blessings we still have. God may have something very wonderful for us waiting around the corner," Ruth opined.

"I thought you were of the religious mind that God helps those who help themselves, and it is not predestined what our life will be," Ruthie argued.

"You missed your calling, Ruthie. You should have been a lawyer, since you seem to enjoy the opposite point of view frequently. Maybe Attorney Smithler would take you into his office and train you for the law. You can still do that in New York State, you know, and all you would have to do is carry a briefcase all about!" Ruth said in a sarcastic tone.

Both women fell silent and looked at each other intensely.

Ruth finally broke the silence, "Okay, Ruthie, let us examine what has happened to me in the past twelve years. I lose a job to a man because he has a family to support and he is a veteran. Teaching was all I really knew. I had been a good teacher and loved my subject matter. My parents are both dead. I had a house, but it had to be sold because, without a job, I knew it would go into foreclosure. I cannot begin to tell you how depressed I was. But soon, my cousin Billy was calling me and saying you needed help taking care of your mother. I had met you once at our Packer family reunion, remember? I was attracted to you the first time I met you. You were tall, attractive, very well spoken and so physically fit, and your eyes were filled with much tenderness. We briefly visited that day at the reunion. You wanted to know all about me and what I was doing with my life. Being four years your junior, I was headed off to college just then and you were very excited for me. It was obvious you did not think the world revolved around you. So, when Billy called me about moving to Four Corners soon after I had sold the only home I had known, I jumped at the chance. A new pathway soon revealed itself as we fell in love, became companions, and created a life for ourselves. Before a year was out, I had a new teaching position in Four Corners working for a principal who wanted to promote my career, not stop it. And that is just what he has done for me, for us, with this promotion.

"Now, I suppose you could say all of this was serendipitous, but I think it was God shining a light down that new pathway and asking me to have the courage to go. God does not have us on puppet strings. We are given free will. However, it is up to us to trust and go down that pathway He may have lighted for us. We can resist the journey, but the outcome will not be as good. So, my best friend, my lover, my soul mate, as they are saying these days, what will it be for you?" Ruth earnestly inquired.

As Ruthie fell silent, Ruth kissed her good night and walked out the door. Ruth was the only person on the face of the earth that could leave Ruthie speechless. Ruth did not have to be cruel to get her point across. She always made Ruthie look at a difficult situation with a perspective that was realistic but tinged with hopefulness. Maybe it was time to think about all the positive things that could happen for them if the farm was sold.

⸺

Ruth had just arrived home from the hospital. It was Friday night of the third week Ruthie had been hospitalized. She was in the process of feeding Jenny when she heard a car pull into the driveway. Upon looking out the door window, she could see it was June's car. June was neatly dressed in a brown wool blazer and matching slacks with an oatmeal-colored turtleneck. Happiness and fear filled her mind as she watched June confidently walk to the door. She looked very "preppy" and comely. Ruth did not wait for June to knock but immediately opened the door.

"This is a pleasant surprise," Ruth commented as June walked by her, dropping a paper bag on the kitchen table.

"Yes, I suppose I should have called first, but I just felt the need to come here and see if you are all right and if there is anything I might be able to do to help," June said. "I have missed seeing you in the faculty lounge at noon. I know you explained to me you needed that time in your office to do lesson plans for the next day now that you stop by the hospital to see Ruthie every night. I thought maybe a Jake's Diner sandwich, along with some of Jake's special apple pie, might be of use tonight, and I could get caught up with a health report on Ruthie," June said.

"How did you know I hadn't eaten supper yet?" Ruth remarked. "How kind that you thought of me and dropped by with some sustenance. I can make a fresh pot of coffee. Here, have a seat while I get the coffee brewing and finish feeding Jenny," Ruth suggested.

"Poor old Jenny," June exclaimed. "She must really miss Ruthie. Too bad you can't sneak her into the hospital so that she knows Ruthie is alive!"

"Oh, I am pretty sure she understands Ruthie is just away for a while. Every day when I head out the door, I try to remember to take an extra handkerchief to put in Ruthie's hand while I visit her. When I get home, I tell Jenny her "mommy" is okay and give her the handkerchief. On some level, she knows what has happened because she always comes up to me and lays her head on my lap when I tell her that," Ruth explained.

June smiled and shook her head. "You are a wonder. You think of everything, like bringing Ruthie's scent home with you. Instead of saying thanks for a sandwich you use the word *sustenance*. That's why I find you so charming," June said.

Ruth looked to the counter and watched the coffee percolate as she considered whether June had just given her a well-intentioned compliment or a flirtation. It was late to be stopping by with supper at 9:30, and manners would have dictated a phone call first. Truthfully, Ruth was happy for the company. She grabbed the coffeepot and poured them both a steaming cup of coffee. "It will be nice to eat supper with someone other than Jenny. We take so many things in our daily life for granted until one of those things disappears, as in eating every supper with Ruthie. Thanks for the food and the company," Ruth replied.

The two women chatted about Ruthie's health and all the latest events at school as they ate the delicious sandwiches and consumed the pie and coffee.

June caught Ruth staring at the kitchen clock, realizing it was almost 11:30. She knew she should leave. "I see two hours have flown by, and I better get going so you can get some rest after another long week," June remarked. She rose to her feet and turned toward the door.

Ruth agreed it had been a long week and expressed her thanks that tomorrow was Saturday. As she opened the door to let June leave, June asked her if it was okay to give her a hug. "I can always use a hug," Ruth replied.

Before she knew it, June enfolded her strong arms around her, and for a moment, it felt like one of Ruthie's loving hugs, which she had missed for several months now. Ruth began to tear up, which did not go unnoticed by June. "I didn't intend for you to cry, Ruth. I'm sorry."

"Don't be sorry, friend. As you say, it has been a long week and your hug just reminds me how much I miss Ruthie," Ruth explained as she wiped her eyes with her apron.

June said good night and quickly got in her car.

Ruth put the dishes in the sink and headed up to bed with the ever faithful and arthritic Jenny limping behind. As she settled into bed with Jenny, Ruth thought about the past two hours with June. She admitted to herself there was some chemistry between them. She also knew June's hug was just that, a hug from June, not a hug from Ruthie, to whom she had given her heart a long time ago.

Chapter 17

Ruthie was released from the hospital to the farmhouse a month after admission. She moved about very cautiously using a cane but was ever so grateful for the only home she had known for forty-four years. Jenny was so happy to see Ruthie that Ruth had to restrain the dog so as not to knock Ruthie down. Ruthie had come to accept the fact she would never be able to farm again according to her doctor. She had signed a real estate agreement with Billy to sell the farm and cattle, as well as all the farm equipment, for $35,000. In return, Billy had agreed to let Ruthie and Ruth stay in the farmhouse for six months while they located new lodging near the school district. Eventually, Billy and Cindy would occupy the former Stein home.

Before Ruthie got home, Cindy had helped Ruth move all Ruthie's clothes, as well as the curtains and matching linens from Ruth's bedroom to the first-floor bedroom, so no stair climbing would be required. Billy had installed a shower in the downstairs bathroom, indicating that this would be something he and Cindy would use regularly when they moved in later. No explanation about sleeping arrangements for Ruth was needed for their dear friends, Cindy and Billy. Cindy had even prepared dinner for Ruthie's first night home, and the four friends ate together with Ruthie staying out of the conversation. Billy and Cindy did not stay long after dinner, knowing Ruth and Ruthie had much to discuss.

Ruthie looked exhausted, and Ruth suggested an early bedtime. "It will be so wonderful to have you next to me again, sweetheart.

I have missed you so," Ruth said as she dropped her arms around Ruthie's shoulders and kissed her on the cheek.

"I am quite certain it will be a different woman you will be sleeping next to tonight," Ruthie replied as she used the kitchen table to rise to her feet.

"What do you mean by that comment?" Ruth asked with a voice full of uncertainty.

"I simply mean I feel very battered; very old; and, as they say these days, out of my element," Ruthie muttered.

"Maybe I can help you feel a little better, and I'm not talking about passionate lovemaking. You still love me, don't you? Hopefully that hasn't changed, has it? I need you, Ruthie," Ruth said.

"Of course, I still love you. I am just trying to figure out how you could possibly need me. You are making more money than I ever dreamed of providing for you. You are still the beautiful woman I welcomed into my home twelve years ago. I, on the other hand, am physically broken down, and I can no longer provide any income. You told me years ago that my physical strength and stature was so attractive to you. Well, I can't even stand for very long now," Ruthie said with an edge to her voice.

"Now that's enough self-pity," Ruth sternly commanded. "Look, I know you have been through so much. You've had excruciating physical pain for a month, and you rarely complained about that pain. Your injury has also deprived you of your vocation as a farmer, and now you are about to move out of your family home. That is too much all at one time for anyone to endure. But you have told me many times over the past twelve years that your life, even this farm, had no real meaning until you had me in your life. I am standing right here in front of you. I am still here, and you cannot speak for me about why I need you as much as ever," Ruth snapped as tears came to her eyes.

Ruthie opened her mouth to speak but realized she didn't know what to say. She had been holding onto the side of the kitchen table for stability but let go and reached for Ruth. Ruth stepped forward and put her arms around Ruthie, so she wouldn't stumble. "I guess you are stronger than I thought," Ruthie said with a smile as she straightened up and put her arms firmly around Ruth, giving her as strong a hug as she could muster. They stood silently hugging each other for a long time.

Once in the bedroom, Ruth helped Ruthie get into her nightgown and into their bed, placing the cane by Ruthie's side of the bed. Once comfortably settled in bed, the two women held hands and drifted off to sleep.

As the morning sun broke through the blue curtains, Ruthie awakened, as had been her custom her entire life. She lay next to Ruth and watched her steady breathing. It was a Saturday, so Ruth could sleep in an extra hour. She thought about the things she had said last night as she'd whined about having nothing to give Ruth. It hurt to hear it, but Ruth was right when she had accused her of self-pity. Ruth's love for her was a blessing and not something she could earn. Her pride had been hurt by the events of the past month. To feel worthy of real love, Ruthie always thought she had to gain it by being strong and taking care of everyone else.

She slipped out of bed, grabbed her cane, and left the room to prepare breakfast. She still knew how to make good scrambled eggs. Her secret to making this famous breakfast treat was putting in just a little cream and cheese. Ruth had complimented Ruthie on her coffee-making skills many times. "Not too strong, and not too weak," Ruth would say and then add, "I wish I could make coffee like this!" Ruthie had noticed last night a loaf of Bessie Packer's homemade bread, which would make delicious toast. How wonderful it was to be free of hospital food.

When the eggs were almost fully cooked, Ruthie pulled the iron skillet off the burner, popped the bread in the toaster, and headed to the bedroom to awaken Ruth.

Ruth was sitting on the side of the bed trying to wake up. When she saw Ruthie, she smiled. "Do I smell some of your delicious coffee, sweetheart? Gosh I've missed those times when you would get in from the barn before I got up on weekends and make that sacred brew," Ruth said.

When Ruth got to the kitchen and noticed Ruthie had set the table and made breakfast, she knew Ruthie had ended the self-pity, for now at least. Ruthie pulled out Ruth's chair for her and said, "Welcome to the Stein diner. Some scrambled eggs and toast for you madam?" she inquired.

"That would be just the ticket, along with some famous Stein coffee," Ruth replied.

The two women slowly ate their breakfast while Ruth reported all the latest news from the church and school.

Ruthie asked, "How about June? How's her love life these days? Did she drop in to see you while I was in the hospital?"

Ruth didn't want to recall that evening when June had unexpectedly popped in, but there was no reason to lie about it because nothing had happened except for a lingering hug. "She came by one Friday evening and brought a sandwich and some pie from Jake's Diner for a late supper. She wanted to get the real scoop on your diagnosis and see if there was anything she could do to help me," Ruth explained as she crunched down on her last piece of toast.

"I'm sure she did want to know my diagnosis and what she could do for you," Ruthie replied with a laugh and a smile. "You know, she came by the hospital twice. First time, she wanted to know how we were coping with this dilemma and if I wanted her to stay at the farm with you to help while I was recuperating in the hospital. I told her she would have to ask you about that but that I believed Billy was watching out for you, as well as all the farm chores," Ruthie said.

"You can't be serious!" Ruth replied. "How presumptuous of her! That really offends me!"

"Don't worry about it, my dear. I knew what you would say to that proposal should she actually get up the courage to ask," Ruthie assured Ruth. "I am the jealous type, I admit. June is quite attractive and quite obviously stuck on you. But I have come to learn over these past twelve years that, if there is just one person in the world I can trust, it is you. And if I can't trust you, who could I trust?" Ruthie smiled.

"And on her second visit, what did she say?" Ruth asked.

"It was quite different during her second visit. She brought in some flowers and indicated she was so sad I had to stay so long in the hospital. She went on to say that it might not seem like it, but despite it all, I was the luckiest woman in the world to have you in my life. She told me about stopping by that Friday night, and through your tears, she could see how devoted you were to me," Ruthie said.

"Well, she is quite right about that, sweetheart. I don't know what June hoped to accomplish during your hospitalization, but she does not hold a candle to you in any respect," Ruth said with authority.

"I had a lot of time to reflect on just that, the last few days in the hospital. I also thought a lot about our housing arrangements when we move from this farmhouse. We could rent, but owning a small, one-story home with no mortgage, would make us more secure. I have already called Attorney Smithler about writing my will and leaving everything, including the house, to you. That would make me feel like I was really contributing to our life together," Ruthie reasoned.

"That is a very generous offer, Ruthie, but I can't let you do that. We should not use any of the farm sale to buy a home. The whole amount you receive for the farm should go into a savings account in your name for retirement purposes. Maybe you are also overlooking the hefty medical bills from the doctors and the month-long hospital stay?"

"This time, I am one step ahead of you," Ruthie began. "Before I left the hospital, I asked to see the administrator and asked him to estimate what would be my medical costs. He told me that the cost of my private room was $50 a day, and since I had been in the hospital a month, that would add up to be about $1,500. As for the surgical procedures and doctor bills, I should expect a bill about $2,000.

Altogether that is about $3,500. Having paid my parent's hospital bills in years past, I knew my bill would be hefty. Hearing that figure was what really convinced me to sell the farm," she explained.

"Doesn't that also convince you of the need to save the farm sale proceeds for retirement and that we can rent and not buy right now?" Ruth replied.

"You need to understand, Ruth, that this is a serious matter to me. I need to feel as if I am really your lifetime companion by doing my fair share to keep us financially sound. After paying off the medical bills, it would be wiser financially to purchase a small home. Who knows if I will be able to find any kind of job around here? I learned to type in high school. I can fix farm equipment. Who would have need of those skills from a woman living in Four Corners?" Ruthie argued.

"You are underestimating yourself, Ruthie. You never know what God has around the corner for you in the form of a new vocation. Maybe it is time for you to go back to school?" Ruth suggested.

"You can't be serious! I am forty-four years old, and just what do you suggest I study?" Ruthie retorted.

"Don't be so startled, Ruthie. You know Jefferson Community College just opened its doors last year, and a whole new campus just off the interstate in Watertown is under construction. They offer accounting courses, which is just up your alley. You have kept impeccable farm records for years, and you have an unusually keen mind for math. Businesses are always looking for bookkeepers or accountants," Ruth persisted.

"I would be more than twice the age of all the students. They don't want some old lady in their classes," Ruthie said with scorn.

"Who cares what they want or what they think!" Ruth shouted in exasperation. "I doubt you will be the only older student. I may be wrong, but I can see many people going back to school in midlife now. Lots of people wanted to go to college but couldn't afford it unless they were well off or were men who have the GI Bill. Tuition is minimal at the community college, and we certainly could afford that for you."

"We'll see about that," Ruthie groused. "First, we need to find a new place to live. I've been looking in *The Times* real estate section, and it looks like the Taylors have their three-bedroom home on the market for $15,900. We went there one time for a Women's Fellowship meeting a couple years ago, remember? It is a one-story built in 1950. It is better to buy a newer home, rather than some old broken-down farmhouse like this one. We won't have to pay out as much in exterior repairs. Yes, it will be tough to move because this was my family home, and our first twelve years together began right here. This house is filled with many memories, good and bad. But I can move on, and I will. The Taylor place is on a whole acre, giving room for a big garden and even some room for a few chickens. That would keep me busy!" Ruthie reasoned.

"I suppose you are right about buying and not renting. The house should be in your name. What you decide to do with it after you die is your decision. If you need to do this to feel more equal in our companionship, I understand, and I will be thankful always to share the home with you. However, you must accept my teaching and vice principal salary to pay for most of our other costs," Ruth insisted.

"I will try to do that graciously, but it is hard for me, as you know. I don't know how well I will do being a kept woman." Ruthie laughed.

"You kept me for a long time, and now I get to keep you. That is what lifelong sweethearts do, right?" Ruth replied with a twinkle in her eye.

"All I know is that I will always be at home no matter where we go, if you continue to give me your heart," Ruthie said.

With those words, Ruthie walked to Ruth's side of the table, took her hand, and raised Ruth to her feet. Ruthie gathered Ruth into her arms once again and gave her a kiss, which reminded Ruth of their first year together when their love was so new. Both women understood that there would always be a way forward so long as these hugs were never taken for granted.

Printed in the United States
By Bookmasters